THE DRAMA AND MAJESTY OF THE Second COMING

THE DRAMA AND MAJESTY OF THE Second COMING

CLAY McCONKIE, PhD

CFI
SPRINGVILLE, UTAH

ISBN 13: 978-1-59955-279-8

Published by CFI, an imprint of Cedar Fort, Inc., 2373 W. 700 S., Springville, UT 84663
Distributed by Cedar Fort, Inc., www.cedarfort.com

LIBRARY OF CONGRESS CATALOGING-IN-PUBLICATION DATA

McConkie, Clay.
The drama and majesty of the Second Coming / Clay McConkie.
p. cm.
Includes bibliographical references.
ISBN 978-1-59955-279-8
1. Second Advent. 2. Millennium (Eschatology) 3. Church of Jesus Christ
of Latter-day Saints—Doctrines. I. Title.

BX8643.S43M32 2009
236'.9—dc22

2009043195

Cover design by Megan Whittier
Cover design © 2010 by Lyle Mortimer

Printed in the United States of America

10 9 8 7 6 5 4 3 2 1

Printed on acid-free paper

CONTENTS

*"Wherefore, be faithful, praying always,
having your lamps trimmed and burning, and oil with you,
that you may be ready at the coming of the Bridegroom—
For behold, verily, verily, I say unto you, that I come quickly.
Even so. Amen."*

Doctrine and Covenants 33:17–18

INTRODUCTION

One day, on a commercial tour in Israel, the Jewish conductor made an interesting comment. It seemed to be in jest, yet maybe not. He said that when the Messiah comes in the future, there is an important question he wants to ask: "Sir, is this your first visit, or your second?"

It was a humorous comment, but it is true that the Hebrew and Jewish nations have waited for a messiah for centuries. Christians today are also waiting—not for a first visit, but for a second.

Beyond the Atonement and Resurrection, certainly nothing is more prominent or important in Christian belief than the Second Coming of Jesus Christ. Even before Christ left Palestine long ago, people were inquiring about when he would come again: "And as he sat upon the mount of Olives, the disciples came unto him privately, saying, Tell us, when shall these things be? And what shall be the sign of thy coming, and of the end of the world?" (Matthew 24:3). But rather than answer directly, Christ only mentioned things that would happen first, including countless wars and rumors of wars: "For nation shall rise against nation, and kingdom against kingdom: and there shall be famines, and pestilences, and earthquakes, in divers places. . . .

And this gospel of the kingdom,"—or the gospel he introduced during his ministry—"shall be preached in all the world for a witness unto all nations; and then shall the end come" (24:7, 14).

The last statement concerning the preaching of the gospel is especially significant and is reminiscent of the scripture in the Book of Revelation, where it says that an angel will "fly in the midst of heaven, having the everlasting gospel to preach unto them that dwell on the earth, and to every nation, and kindred, and tongue, and people" (14:6).

The "everlasting gospel," of course, means not only the teachings of Jesus Christ during the meridian of time but also the message of prophets throughout the course of history, beginning with Adam and continuing periodically for four thousand years. The primary message, and the meaning behind countless sacrifices that were made upon ancient altars, was that a savior would be born who would someday perform a personal, infinite sacrifice known as the Atonement. The truth of this singular event was what was to be proclaimed to all nations of the earth.

The worldwide preaching of the gospel, in fact, is one of the key signs that is to come before the Second Coming of Jesus Christ. It will be part of the grand sequence of events that leads to Christ's appearance and to the beginning of the Millennium. Along with many other signs, it will introduce the denouement of all human history in the last days and the ultimate climax at the end of the world.

Indeed, the preparations for this final event are beginning to take place. Through the ministering of angels—not just one, but many—the world is finally being prepared for the Second Coming. Every necessary thing is being provided for the entrance of a King. One by one, religious prophecies are being fulfilled, and the world and its many populations stand on the threshold of the greatest event that has ever transpired upon the earth, second only to the Resurrection and the Atonement of Jesus Christ!

Now at the beginning of the seventh millennium, six thousand years after the time of Adam and Eve, according to the present-day calendar, things are already well on their way toward the start of the thousand years known as *the* Millennium. In just the last two centuries, after a long period of time during which there was no recorded revelation, the heavens have once again been opened, and men have claimed to have seen angels and received communication from God. Despite a common belief that there are no longer prophets of old like Abraham, Moses, and Elijah, heavenly beings have again appeared to men during the latter days and the waning hours of time.

These events are reminiscent of older times, when people were more apt to believe in religious miracles and spiritual things. They are comparable to those events that occurred when the world was still relatively new and before mankind was confronted with so many secular ideologies, a time when "by the ministering of angels, and by every word which proceeded forth out of the mouth of God, men began to exercise faith in Christ; and thus by faith, they did lay hold upon every good thing" (Moroni 7:25).

Even in today's modern society, things have definitely changed! After people have been conditioned for years to believe that recorded revelation ceased with the final pages of the Bible, angels, sent from the presence of God, have appeared once more to instruct mankind and prepare them for the future. Heavenly beings have come to introduce a new dispensation of the gospel. During this dispensation, people throughout the world can view what lies ahead with confidence and assurance—if they choose to do so—as they await the Second Coming of Jesus Christ!

1

Six Millennia of the Gospel

In the first four millennia of human history, God spoke to mankind personally from time to time but more often through angels sent from his presence. Such was the case in Adam's time (before and after his expulsion from the Garden of Eden), in the days of Enoch and the prophet Noah, during the period of Abraham and Moses, and throughout biblical times.

Yet even though God spoke to the people, always advocating a gospel plan, only a very small minority listened. It was characteristic of this early history that once God had revealed his will, mankind soon strayed from it and became wayward. The divine plan was for people to gather together and abide by correct principles, but mankind's general inclination was to scatter abroad and go in different directions.

By the time of Jesus, the lost sheep of the house of Israel he had specifically been sent to teach had strayed so far from the truth that he established a new system for preaching the gospel by organizing a church and ordaining twelve apostles. He commissioned these men to begin anew and reestablish the kingdom of God on earth with a relatively new doctrine. Yet in many ways, it was not new but was rather a continuing plan for people to be gathered together so they could hear and obey God's divine will.

1

Throughout the dispensations, prophets delivered this message with unmistakable clarity, admonishing people to believe in the Son of God—the future Messiah who would be born in the meridian of time and would be resurrected following his infinite Atonement and death. All nations were invited to repent and be baptized in the name of the Father, and of the Son, and of the Holy Ghost, consenting to be gathered together and to believe in the saving power of Jesus Christ. In regard to the people in Jerusalem, Jesus said, "O Jerusalem, Jerusalem, thou that killest the prophets, and stonest them which are sent unto thee, how often would I have gathered thy children together, even as a hen gathereth her chickens under her wings, and ye would not!" (Matthew 23:37).

Certainly, this story occurred throughout history and was repeated again and again, people hearing the gospel message but only a very small minority accepting it. This was particularly noticeable during the two thousand years following Jesus' life, when there was a dearth of revelation and recorded scripture. It is no surprise that much of this time period was eventually called the Dark Ages. In reality, there is no reliable explanation for this long interim during which a curtain seemed to be drawn between earth and heaven. In a very short time, the doctrine and ordinances pertaining to Jesus, the early apostles, and those who came after them underwent significant change. Consequently, an apostasy occurred that resulted in an almost innumerable amount of Christian churches. Someone occasionally had some kind of vision or unusual manifestation, but anything that resulted in the type of religious system Jesus had organized, one which included the concept of apostles and continuing revelation, never took place.

At the end of the year 1800, as time continued to draw closer to the Lord's Second Coming, various signs of the times appeared. In the religiously fervid situation of that time, it was inevitable that something new would eventually occur and that there would be some kind of change or transformation. Something different was about to happen that would set the stage for the Second Advent and fulfill religious prophecy. This was the exact point in history, in fact, when the right confluence of conditions and circumstances finally removed the curtain between earth and heaven and initiated a consequent ministering of angels.

2

THE MINISTERING OF ANGELS

During the spring of 1820, in a backwoods area of western New York, a fourteen-year-old boy went into a grove near his home to pray. He had never said a vocal prayer before, but on this occasion he wanted an answer to a very important question—one that he apparently felt required more than the usual, silent prayer.

A religious revival was taking place in his neighborhood at the time, and ministers of many different churches were competing for people to join their respective organizations. The boy's mother, brother, and two of his sisters had already joined a particular church, but he, being conscientious about the matter, was still undecided.

And so, on an early spring day, he knelt in prayer and began to address God in a way he had never done before. There is no doubt that he had the faith he needed, because after reading and studying the Bible, he felt sure he had the right to ask his question. He merely wanted to know which church he should join. If not his mother's church, which other should it be?

As he prayed that morning, he knew he would get some kind of answer, yet the possibility that he was about to have a vision probably never crossed his mind. Never would he have expected more than the normal reply that reading the Bible had prepared him for. It would not have been too unusual for him to receive some type of feeling or manifestation or maybe even some kind of sign. He could then leave the grove knowing for certain which church was the right one.

But on this occasion, much more was involved than just a young man saying a prayer. What was about to happen was much more significant than anyone could possibly have known, because it had never happened before. Nothing in the Bible could have prepared anyone, especially a boy of that age, for what took place. For in the grove that day, as he knelt in prayer, two heavenly beings suddenly appeared before him, one calling him by name and then introducing the other, who finally answered the boy's question.

What happened on that occasion was not just a ministering of angels, though that would happen at a later time, but was a much more significant event. Again it was something that had never taken place previously, and an account of it is best described in the boy's own words.

"I saw two Personages," he said, "whose brightness and glory defy all description, standing above me in the air. One of them spake unto me, calling me by name and said, pointing to the other—This is my beloved Son. Hear Him!" (Joseph Smith History 1:17).

The boy then asked which church he should join, and the answer was that he should join none of them. "They draw near to me with their lips," he was told, "but their hearts are far from me, they teach for doctrines the commandments of men, having a form of godliness, but they deny the power thereof" (Joseph Smith History 1:19).

He learned many other things at the time, after which the vision ended and the two personages disappeared. A question had been asked, and an answer was given. Yet, as the young boy left the grove, he knew much more than what his church membership should be. For the first time, he knew for a certainty who God was and who his

Son was. And regardless of how he had visualized them previously, he realized that they had bodies much like his own and that he could speak with them, much as he could with his own father.

The boy was a different person as he left the grove that day, and he must have sensed that he would have an unusual lifetime ahead of him. Never would he be the same as before, and regardless of what happened, his mind was now at ease and he could marvel at what had taken place. He said of the experience, "I had seen a vision. I knew it, and I knew God knew it, and I could not deny it." And even though there would be many who would question it, he had nevertheless seen a light beyond the brightness of the sun, "and in the midst of that light [he] had seen two personages who did in reality speak to [him]" (Joseph Smith History 1:25). Certainly it was an almost unbelievable experience for such a young man.

The boy's name was Joseph Smith. He lived with his family in a farming community and had very little formal education, but he had a desire for knowledge and was especially inclined toward things that were religious. It is not surprising, therefore, that three years later he had another vision. This heavenly manifestation turned out to be a literal opening of the heavens that had been prophesied—one in which for several years he received the ministration of an angel!

The vision happened on September 21, 1823, in a small log cabin where the Smith family was living at the time. Joseph was in his room. An account of what happened is again best described in his own words:

> While I was thus in the act of calling upon God, I discovered a light appearing in my room, which continued to increase until the room was lighter than at noonday, when immediately a personage appeared at my bedside, standing in the air, for his feet did not touch the floor.
>
> He had on a loose robe of most exquisite whiteness. It was a whiteness beyond anything earthly I had ever seen; nor do

I believe that any earthly thing could be made to appear so exceedingly white and brilliant. His hands were naked, and his arms also, a little above the wrist; so, also, were his feet naked, as were his legs, a little above the ankles. His head and neck were also bare. I could discover that he had no other clothing on but this robe, as it was open, so that I could see into his bosom. (Joseph Smith History 1:30–31)

In no other place is there a more complete description of an angel who had been sent from the presence of God. The angel soon revealed that his name was Moroni. In mortality he had lived in the Americas during the fifth century B.C. He was the son of a man named Mormon and, among other things, was a military commander who had fought in a final battle in which most of his people were killed. The vision then continued:

Not only was his robe exceedingly white, but his whole person was glorious beyond description, and his countenance truly like lightning. The room was exceedingly light, but not so very bright as immediately around his person. When I first looked upon him, I was afraid; but the fear soon left me.

He called me by name and said unto me that he was a messenger sent from the presence of God, and that his name was Moroni; that God had a work for me to do; and that my name should be had for good and evil among all nations, kindreds, and tongues, or that it should be both good and evil spoken of among all people. (Joseph Smith History 1:32–33)

Having given this much information to the boy, Moroni then explained why he had come. He said that a book of metal plates containing a history of the former inhabitants on the American continent was deposited in the ground of a nearby hill. Buried with the plates were two stones in silver bows that were attached to a breastplate. These stones and breastplate were called a Urim and Thummim. Moroni said that "the possession and use of these stones were what constituted 'seers' in ancient or former times" and that God had prepared them for the purpose of Joseph eventually translating the book. He then quoted several scriptures from the Old Testament, commenting on some of them and saying that certain prophecies would soon be fulfilled (see Joseph Smith History 1:34–41).

The account of Joseph Smith going to the hill the following day and finding the plates is well known, as is the fact that they were eventually translated and published as the Book of Mormon. But the important thing that transpired was that an angel had appeared to a man on earth and delivered an important message from God. Following the event that had taken place in the grove three years earlier, Moroni's visit was the next known appearance of a heavenly being, and it was preparatory to many events that would follow. Indeed, it fulfilled the prophecy that an angel would fly through the midst of heaven, having the everlasting gospel to preach unto the inhabitants of the earth (see Revelation 14:6). But above everything else, it was the long-awaited ministering of angels that literally opened the heavens and prepared the way for the Second Coming of Christ!

❧ 3 ❧

A CONTINUING SAGA

It was four years after the appearance of Moroni that Joseph Smith was finally able to take the ancient plates from the ground and begin translating them. During those four years, he was occasionally visited by Moroni, who ministered unto him and gave him further instructions. Joseph was eventually assisted in the translation by a young school teacher named Oliver Cowdery. It was an interesting experience for both of the men, and together they were to have an experience equal to the appearance of Moroni itself.

During the translation, Joseph would read and interpret the Egyptian-like characters through the Urim and Thummim and then dictate them to Oliver, who would record them on paper. Page after page, they completed the record that is now the Book of Mormon. After considerable time had passed, however, the men encountered several references to baptism for the remission of sins, and they wondered how this religious ordinance was relevant to them personally.

Undoubtedly, they were acquainted with the story of Nicodemus in the Bible. He visited Jesus one night, and during their conversation, Nicodemus learned that unless a person is born again, he would not be able to see the kingdom of God. He asked Jesus at that time how a man could be born again when he is old. Could he enter a second time into his mother's womb? Then Jesus explained, "Verily, verily, I say unto thee, Except a man be born of water and of the Spirit, he cannot enter into the kingdom of God" (John 3:5).

This classic scripture prompted Joseph and Oliver to go into the woods one spring day near Joseph's home by the Susquehanna River. Again, it was just a simple prayer, and they might not have expected more than a traditional answer, but once again a heavenly being appeared, descending in a cloud of light and placing his hands upon the two men.

The being identified himself as the resurrected John the Baptist and said he was acting under the direction of the ancient apostles Peter, James, and John who held the Melchizedek Priesthood. By way of a sacred ordinance and the laying on of hands, he conferred priesthood authority that had long been absent from the earth upon Joseph and Oliver.

"Upon you my fellow servants, in the name of Messiah," he said, "I confer the Priesthood of Aaron, which holds the keys of the ministering of angels, and of the gospel of repentance, and of baptism by immersion for the remission of sins; and this shall never be taken again from the earth until the sons of Levi do offer again an offering unto the Lord in righteousness" (D&C 13:1).

The angel then commanded the two men to go to the nearby river and baptize each other by immersion. They later conferred the Aaronic Priesthood on each other, again by the laying on of hands. It was a solemn occasion for them, and for the first time in many centuries, the authority to baptize was once more upon the earth, the administrator of this sacred ordinance being John the Baptist himself!

Logically, there was no one except one person who could have represented God on this occasion. Only the man referred to in the New Testament as the voice of one crying in the wilderness would be the appropriate individual, the one who anciently told the people in Judea to prepare the way of the Lord and make his paths straight. Indeed it was this prophet who came out of the desert in a "raiment of camel's hair, and a leathern girdle about his loins" (Matthew 3:4) and commenced preaching the baptism of repentance for the remission of sins. And it was he who, as a resurrected being sent from the presence of God, now appeared to two men upon the earth.

The restoration of the Aaronic Priesthood on this occasion was unique in that it not only involved the process of baptism and the laying on of hands but that it also involved the ministering of a resurrected being. To the Christian world, as well as beyond, this should have been an event of tremendous importance. In reality, it is a stumbling block for many, since people are not easily convinced that heavenly messengers have appeared during modern times. Just as many believe that there is no scripture beyond what is found in the Bible, many feel that any report of ministering angels should be considered as either untrue or unreliable.

For Joseph Smith, the appearance of a heavenly personage at this time was undoubtedly no great surprise, though it must have been an overwhelming experience for Oliver Cowdery. Though Oliver was fully convinced that his friend had seen heavenly beings while in the grove and during the visitations of Moroni, he was undoubtedly taken back by his own encounter with an angelic being. Later he described in part what had happened and how he felt: "I shall not attempt to paint to you the feelings of this heart," he said, "nor the majestic beauty and glory which surrounded us on this occasion. The Lord, who is rich in mercy, and is ever willing to answer the consistent prayer of the humble, after we had called him in a fervent manner, aside from the abodes of men, condescended to manifest to us his will. And as we heard we rejoiced, while His love enkindled upon our souls, and we were wrapped in the vision of the Almighty!"[1]

In light of what had happened, it must have been evident to both Oliver and Joseph that they stood on the threshold of outstanding events—events that would accompany the translation and publication of the Book of Mormon and enable them to organize a Church in the near future. The formation of the Church had been forecast earlier in the grove when the Lord informed Joseph that he would be instrumental in establishing a church that would be neither Catholic nor Protestant but, rather, one that was restored from ancient times.

First, it was necessary for Joseph to obtain permission and power to do this by receiving additional priesthood authority. This event took place a short time later, again in the company of Oliver Cowdery near the Susquehanna River. This time, the ancient apostles Peter, James, and John miraculously appeared. They announced themselves as those holding the Melchizedek Priesthood, "possessing the keys of the kingdom, and of the dispensation of the fulness of times" (D&C 128:20). They laid their hands upon the two men, and gave them the additional priesthood authority they would need to organize the church of Jesus Christ upon the earth.

As they did so, they used language reminiscent of words spoken by Peter himself to the people in Palestine, telling them how God would someday perform a miraculous work during the times of restitution—a term synonymous with the dispensation of the fulness of times: "And he shall send Jesus Christ," Peter said, "which before was preached unto you: Whom the heaven must receive until the times of restitution of all things, which God hath spoken by the mouth of all his holy prophets since the world began" (Acts 3:20–21).

Again, it was logical and appropriate for these particular men to restore the Melchizedek Priesthood. They were the ones who, during mortality, accompanied Jesus on many occasions. They were with him on the Mount of Transfiguration, and they waited in the Garden of Gethsemane as he began the Atonement. Together they formed a triumvirate that would constitute a model for ages to come in which three individuals, much like the Godhead itself, would preside over the affairs of the Priesthood.

Consequently, it was Peter, James, and John who conferred upon Joseph Smith and Oliver Cowdery both the authority and the keys of the Melchizedeck priesthood. These three men, all resurrected except John, had been sent from the presence of God as ministering angels to commune with men living on the earth. For many people, this miraculous event would almost be beyond comprehension, and especially in a modern society that is always reaching new levels of science and technology, it would also be a test of faith.

It was also during this same time period that another heavenly visitation took place. This one involved more than just Joseph and Oliver. For more than a year, Oliver had been engaged in translating the ancient record known as the Book of Mormon. Throughout the translation, Joseph had not shown the plates to anyone. As he later recalled, this was a burden and anxiety for him because he knew there were those who questioned whether he actually had the plates. The time came, however, when the record was finally shown to other people. This occasion brought another appearance by Moroni.

First, three men were given the opportunity to view the ancient record: Oliver Cowdery and two others, namely David Whitmer and Martin Harris. They, together with Joseph Smith, retired to the woods one day and, while praying, were visited by Moroni, who held the sacred record in his hands, turning some of the leaves over one by so they could see the engravings.

Later, the three men published a signed testimony of what they had seen, a part of which reads, "And we declare with words of soberness, that an angel of God came down from heaven, and he brought and laid before our eyes, that we beheld and saw the plates, and the engravings thereon; and we know that it is by the grace of God the Father, and our Lord Jesus Christ, that we beheld and bear record that these things are true. And it is marvelous in our eyes" (Testimony of the Three Witnesses).

Now, having received the proper priesthood authority and having completed the work of translation, Joseph Smith organized a church—not one of his own making, but one that had existed anciently during the ministry of Jesus Christ. It was the Church he had prayed to find in the grove several years ago. It was a church in which people were baptized by immersion for the remission of sins, and received the gift of the Holy Ghost by the laying on of hands. It was an organization that was soon to have apostles like those in the primitive church, all acting under the authority of Peter, James, and John.

Once again, this new organization had no connection with any church that was Protestant, Catholic, Jewish, or any other denomination. It was restored in the final stages of time, preparatory to the second coming of Christ and the beginning of the Millennium. Its restoration was predicted by prophets of old, who said it would come in the times of restitution and in the dispensation of the fulness of times. Indeed, it was a church that had come out of the wilderness, and it was the Church of Jesus Christ in the latter days!

This was a significant mark in time, not only for Joseph Smith but for anyone living in this period. During the final dispensation of the gospel, when all of the religious principles and doctrines of past ages were to be restored to the earth, something new and different needed to happen—something that would establish a new system of religious living and prepare the way for the Second Coming. It would include such things as a radically new concept of Deity and of the Godhead, the restoration of valid priesthood authority, an additional set of ancient and modern scripture to accompany and complement the Bible, and sacred temples that would eventually dot the world.

It was, without question, the most revolutionary and significant expression of spirituality that had occurred since the time of Jesus. In an unprecedented confluence of ministering angels, the untainted gospel of former times was restored to the earth, and the church of God was established. Living prophets and apostles, all possessing what was called the Melchizedek Priesthood, presided over a worldwide network of congregations. Once more, mankind was introduced to the idea of divine revelation, and on many different occasions the heavens were literally opened!

Joseph Smith summarized many of these events in a modern book of scripture called the Doctrine and Covenants. He also recorded some of the angelic visitations he received during that time:

> Now, what do we hear in the gospel which we have received? A voice of gladness! A voice of mercy from heaven; and a voice of truth out of the earth; glad tidings for the dead; a voice of gladness for the living and the dead; glad tidings of great joy. . . .
>
> And again, what do we hear? Glad tidings from Cumorah! Moroni, an angel from heaven, declaring the fulfilment of the prophets—the book to be revealed. A voice of the Lord in the wilderness of Fayette, Seneca county, declaring the three witnesses to bear record of the book! The voice of Michael on the banks of the Susquehanna, detecting the devil when he appeared as an angel of light! The voice of Peter, James, and John in the wilderness between Harmony, Susquehanna county, and Colesville, Broome county, on the Susquehanna River, declaring themselves as possessing the keys of the kingdom, and of the dispensation of the fulness of times!
>
> And again, the voice of God in the chamber of old Father Whitmer, in Fayette, Seneca county, and at sundry times, and in divers places through all the travels and tribulations of this Church of Jesus Christ of Latter-day Saints! And the voice of Michael, the archangel; the voice of Gabriel, and of Raphael, and of divers angels, from Michael or Adam down to the present time, all declaring their dispensation, their rights, their keys, their honors, their majesty and glory, and the power of their priesthood; giving line upon line, precept upon precept; here a little, and there a little; giving us consolation by holding forth that which is to come, confirming our hope! (D&C 128:19–21)

The historic ministering of angels, therefore, whether it be in person or only by voice, has been a continuing saga in the latter days and will continue until the end of the world and the beginning of the Millennium. It is destined to end only when the curtain of heaven is unfolded and the face of the Lord is revealed. Certainly nothing can compare with the almost unfathomable events and circumstances yet to come. In the meantime, the memorable saga continues, full of significant events—not the least of which is the occasional visitations by Jehovah himself to his temples!

Notes

1. *Times and Seasons,* vol. 2. Nauvoo, Illinois: The Church of Jesus Christ of Latter-day Saints, 1839–46. 201.

4

JEHOVAH IN THE TEMPLE

In the record of Malachi, the last book in the Old Testament, Malachi refers to a messenger that will someday be sent to earth, preparing the way for the coming of the Lord. Presumably this can be related to the Second Coming, but there might be multiple meanings, including when John the Baptist came during the meridian of time as the messenger before Christ. But Malachi's words also might refer to a time yet to come when the sons of Levi will be purified.

The interesting part of the scripture is where it refers to the Lord suddenly coming to his temple, which does not sound like anything in the New Testament. The many occasions when Jesus visited the temple in Jerusalem during his earthly ministry were generally not very sudden. Malachi's statement clearly speaks of a time during the latter days—a time when people will either be prepared or unprepared to understand the significance and to handle the consequences of the Lord's Second Coming. The scripture states,

> Behold, I will send my messenger, and he shall prepare the way before me: and the Lord, whom ye seek, shall suddenly come to his temple, even the messenger of the covenant, whom ye delight in: behold he shall come, saith the Lord of hosts.

But who may abide the day of his coming? and who shall stand when he appeareth? for he is like a refiner's fire, and like fuller's soap: and he shall sit as a refiner and purifier of silver: and he shall purify the sons of Levi, and purge them as gold and silver, that they may offer unto the Lord an offering in righteousness." (Malachi 3:1–3)

A scriptural definition of *temple* is not easy to come by since the word *temple* technically could denote any number of places or situations. One example is in the book of Genesis, in which Jacob, the grandson of Abraham, had an unusual experience north of the city of Jerusalem. He was on a journey to Mesopotamia at the time and had stopped for the night. What happened there was totally unexpected and was a turning point in his life.

During the night, Jacob had a dream in which a ladder was set up on the earth. The top of it reached to heaven, and angels of God ascended and descended on it. "And, behold, the Lord stood above it, and said, I am the Lord God of Abraham thy father, and the God of Isaac: the land whereon thou liest, to thee will I give it, and to thy seed; And thy seed shall be as the dust of the earth, and thou shalt spread abroad to the west, and to the east, and to the north, and to the south: and in thee and in thy seed shall all the families of the earth be blessed" (Genesis 28:13–14).

Jacob learned other things that night, and when the vision ended, he took a stone and set it up for a pillar, pouring oil on it and sanctifying the spot as a holy and sacred place. "Surely the Lord is in this place," he said, "and I knew it not. How dreadful is this place! this is none other but the house of God, and this is the gate of heaven" (28:16–17).

Before leaving the next morning, Jacob named the place Bethel, a place that would be regarded in the future as a religious shrine. "And this stone, which I have set for a pillar," he said, "shall be God's house" (28:24).

The meaning of *beth* in the name Bethel is "house," and the letters *el* in the Hebrew language signify "Elohim" or "God."

Certainly the place that Jacob visited that night can be considered a temple, and the event which occurred there a revelation from God.

The same might be said of Mount Sinai, where Moses received the Ten Commandments. In a deserted place in the wilderness, he and Aaron, along with two other men and seventy of the elders of Israel, went up toward the mount and saw the Lord. Previously, Moses had built an altar under a nearby hill and erected twelve pillars representing the twelve tribes of Israel. "And they saw the God of Israel: and there was under his feet as it were a paved work of a sapphire stone, and as it were the body of heaven in his clearness" (Exodus 24:10).

It was but a short time later that the Lord told Moses to come to the top of Mount Sinai, where Moses was given the commandments written on tables of stone. In a climb that would forever be etched in history, the prophet did as he was commanded. What took place there is one of the most remarkable instances ever recorded in scripture:

> And Moses went up into the mount, and a cloud covered the mount.
>
> And the glory of the Lord abode upon mount Sinai, and the cloud covered it six days: and the seventh day he called unto Moses out of the midst of the cloud.
>
> And the sight of the glory of the Lord was like devouring fire on the top of the mount in the eyes of the children of Israel.
>
> And Moses went into the midst of the cloud, and gat him up into the mount: and Moses was in the mount forty days and forty nights. (Exodus 24:15–18)

Once again, God spoke to a man who had been called as a prophet and gave him commandments—the place of the event being a temple on a mountaintop. No building was there, but nevertheless it was a place where Deity revealed its presence upon holy ground. The same was also true in a grove of trees in western New York many centuries later, where Joseph Smith sought the answer to a question in earnest prayer. When Joseph prayed that day, it was not in a cathedral or near any church altar, but rather in a secluded place in the wilderness near his home. Yet the place where he knelt, and where God and his Son Jehovah reportedly appeared and spoke to him, was a holy place—none other than a house of God and a gate of heaven.

Similarly, the appearance of heavenly beings can take place in any area or locality where the Spirit of the Lord is present. But in today's modern setting, where society has become more complex and there are many distracting influences, an actual temple like those that existed in ancient Israel might be a more appropriate and likely place. It is in just such a temple during modern times, therefore, that the ministering of angels continued.

Six years after Joseph restored the pristine Church and priesthood authority—including the authority to build a house of God—the members built the first temple of the new dispensation in Kirtland, Ohio. It was a wooden structure that was built through dedication and sacrifice by a small group and was dedicated as a place where the Lord could visit his people and as a place where he might suddenly come to his temple.

The Lord did appear in the Kirtland Temple while Joseph Smith and Oliver Cowdery were kneeling in prayer only a few days after the temple's dedication. Joseph recounted:

> The veil was taken from our minds, and the eyes of our understanding were opened.
>
> We saw the Lord standing upon the breastwork of the pulpit, before us; and under his feet was a paved work of pure gold, in color like amber.
>
> His eyes were as a flame of fire; the hair of his head was white like the pure snow; his countenance shown above the brightness of the sun; and his voice was as the sound of the rushing of great waters, even the voice of Jehovah, saying:

I am the first and the last; I am he who liveth, I am he who was slain; I am your advocate with the Father." (D&C 110:1–4)

The event in the temple on this occasion was the first recorded account in which the Lord appeared and spoke to Oliver Cowdery, and it must have been another overwhelming experience for him. To see the Lord in person and to hear his voice is something that has occurred to very few people. What happened next was almost equal in significance. Three ministering angels appeared, once more described by Joseph Smith: "After this vision closed," Joseph said, "the heavens were again opened unto us; and Moses appeared before us, and committed unto us the keys of the gathering of Israel from the four parts of the earth, and the leading of the ten tribes from the land of the north" (D&C 110:11).

After many centuries, those people who had an Israelite connection and were scattered throughout the world were now to be joined together, depending upon their faith in Jesus Christ and their willingness to be gathered. Also, those of the ten tribes of Israel who disappeared in the north countries hundreds of years before Christ's earthly ministry would now to be brought back from a long seclusion. The priesthood keys, meaning the permission and authority to accomplish this task, were now given to men on earth, this time delivered by Moses, who during his lifetime was responsible for gathering the children of Israel and leading them out of Egyptian bondage.

Following this visitation, the prophet known as Elias appeared and committed to Joseph and Oliver the dispensation of the gospel of Abraham. He addressed them, "saying that in us and our seed all generations after us should be blessed" (D&C 110:12).

It is unknown exactly who Elias was in mortality. "Elias" could have been Abraham, Melchizedek, or some other notable person during that time period, but one thing is certain—it was not the prophet Elijah, who has also been referred to as Elias. In the New Testament account of Jesus being transfigured on the mount, for example, the Greek form of Elijah, "Elias," is used. The Bible says it was Moses and Elias who appeared to Jesus at that time, but in actuality it was Elijah.

In any case, the keys to the dispensation of the gospel of Abraham, which Elias gave to Joseph Smith and Oliver Cowdery, were essentially the same keys and authority that Abraham had during ancient times. These keys related to the promise that in Abraham all nations of the earth would be blessed and that by way of his priesthood, including the sealing power, his posterity would be as numerous as the sands of the sea and of the dust of the earth. Indeed, the keys that Elias restored at this time, although not completely understood by many, were intended to be of great worth to all people who live by the principles and ordinances of the gospel.

After Elias, a third being appeared—Elijah. In regard to him, Joseph wrote:

> After this vision had closed, another great and glorious vision burst upon us; for Elijah the prophet, who was taken to heaven without tasting death, stood before us, and said:
>
> Behold, the time has fully come, which was spoken by the mouth of Malachi—testifying that he (Elijah) should be sent, before the great and dreadful day of the Lord come—
>
> To turn the hearts of the fathers to the children, and the children to the fathers, lest the whole earth be smitten with a curse.
>
> Therefore, the keys of this dispensation are committed into your hands; and by this ye may know that the great and dreadful day of the Lord is near, even at the doors." (D&C 110:13–16)

It is understandably difficult for many people in the world today to accept what happened to Joseph Smith and Oliver Cowdery on this occasion. Following such a long interim during which divine revelation and the recording of scripture did not occur, most people were conditioned to the idea that revelation has ceased and that there was no need for any further scripture.

But it is nevertheless true, according to revelation and in connection with the commonly accepted calendar, that the human family is likely living in the later stages of its history—in the Saturday afternoon of time, as it were. And now, more than ever before, it is possible that the Lord has intervened and is preparing the world for the Second Coming! Angels have appeared, fulfilling ancient prophecy and delivering messages sent from the presence of God. Never before in matters of religion and spirituality has there been such urgency. The final passages of time are coming to an end and "the great and dreadful day of the Lord is near, even at the doors!"

5

A GRANDDAUGHTER'S STORY

When Joseph Smith died, he was succeeded by others, who one by one became the prophet and president of the new restored church. They were assisted by twelve apostles, the first group of whom were appointed during Joseph's lifetime. The intent was to preserve the same organization that existed in the primitive church during the ministry of Jesus, including apostles, prophets, pastors, teachers, and evangelists (Article of Faith 6).

It soon became evident, however, that the visitation of angels had temporarily come to an end. All that was necessary in opening a new dispensation had been accomplished. The Church had been restored along with priesthood authority, new scripture was introduced, and temple building soon commenced. Through the ministering of angels—not just one, but many—the heavens had literally been opened, and a new system of religion was in place in preparation for the Second Coming of Jesus Christ.

Following the time of Joseph Smith, succeeding presidents were reticent about any heavenly manifestations they might have received personally during their administration. It became almost a protocol to keep things of a very sacred nature resigned to the precincts of a temple. This was evident during the lifetime of Lorenzo Snow, the fifth church president, who succeeded

Wilford Woodruff. What happened to him on one occasion might never have come to light had it not been for a conversation he had with a young granddaughter one night in the Salt Lake Temple.

The event that Lorenzo Snow related to his granddaughter happened at a time when Wilford Woodruff was still the president of the Church. President Woodruff was very ill, however, and his health was rapidly deteriorating. Lorenzo Snow was the senior member and president of the twelve apostles at the time, and it was customary for him to visit the President at his home almost every day. On one particular evening, the doctors finally informed him that his friend was failing fast and possibly would not live much longer.

Lorenzo was worried about becoming the new president, especially since the Church was in serious trouble financially at that time. After leaving the President's home that evening, he went to the temple, and what happened there was later described by his son:

> My father went to his room in the Salt Lake Temple where he was residing at the time. He dressed in his robes of the Priesthood, went into the Holy of Holies there in the House of the Lord and knelt at the sacred altar. He pled with the Lord to spare President Woodruff's life, that President Woodruff might outlive him and that the great responsibility of Church leadership would never fall upon his shoulders. Yet he promised the Lord that he would devotedly perform any duty required at his hands. At this time he was in his eighty-sixth year.[1]

A short time later, the ailing president passed away, and the man who would soon assume leadership of the Church went to the temple again:

> President Snow put on his holy temple robes, repaired again to the same sacred altar, offered up the signs of the Priesthood, and poured out his heart to the Lord. He reminded the

Lord how he had pled for President Woodruff's life and that his days might be lengthened beyond his own, that he might never be called upon to bear the heavy burdens of responsibilities of Church leadership. "Nevertheless," he said, "Thy will be done. I have not sought this responsibility, but if it be thy will, I now present myself before Thee for Thy guidance and instruction. I ask that thou show me what thou wouldst have me do."

After finishing his prayer he expected a reply, some special manifestation from the Lord. So he waited—and waited—and waited. There was no reply, no voice, no visitation, no manifestation. He left the altar and the room in great disappointment. He passed through the Celestial Room and out into the large corridor leading to his own room where a most glorious manifestation was given President Snow. One of the most beautiful accounts of this experience is told by his granddaughter, Allie Young Pond.

"One evening when I was visiting Grandpa Snow in his room in the Salt Lake Temple, I remained until the doorkeepers had gone and the night watchman had not yet come in, so grandpa said he would take me to the main front entrance and let me out that way. He got his bunch of keys from his dresser.

"After we left his room and while we were still in the large corridor leading into the Celestial Room, I was walking several steps ahead of grandpa when he stopped me, saying: 'Wait a moment, Allie. I want to tell you something. It was right here that the Lord Jesus Christ appeared to me at the time of the death of President Woodruff. He instructed me to go right ahead and reorganize the First Presidency of the Church at once and not wait as had been done after the death of the previous presidents, and that I was to succeed President Woodruff.'

"Then grandpa came a step nearer and held our his left hand and said: 'He stood right here, about three feet above the floor. It looked as though he stood on a plate of solid gold.'

"Grandpa told me what a glorious person the Savior is and described his hands, feet, countenance and beautiful White Robes, all of which were of such a glory of whiteness and brightness that he could hardly gaze upon him.

"Then grandpa came another step nearer me and put his right hand on my head and said: 'Now, granddaughter, I want you to remember that this is the testimony of your grandfather, that he told you with his own lips that he actually saw the Savior here in the Temple and talked with him face to face.' "[2]

The remarkable experience that Lorenzo Snow had in the temple that day was just another of many instances predicted by the prophet Malachi when he said that the Lord would "suddenly come to his temple." It was an occasion during the latter days when Jehovah himself appeared at a specific time and place to communicate with someone on earth. Moreover, it was one of many instances that are preparatory to a time when Christ will appear in the clouds of heaven, clothed with power and great glory. That future event will be the ultimate climax. The Lord will appear suddenly and unexpectedly, fulfilling all the words of the prophets and coming from his Father's presence and a heavenly temple that exists on high.

Notes

1. N. B. Lundwall (ed.), *Temples of the Most High* (Salt Lake City: Bookcraft), 148–150.

2. Ibid.

6

SEVEN ERAS OF HUMAN HISTORY

One of the most interesting parts of the Book of Revelation tells of a singular and unusual event that reportedly occurred in the temple in heaven, where God was sitting on his throne. Around him were twenty-four seats upon which twenty-four elders sat, all clothed in white robes with golden crowns upon their heads. Thunderings and lightnings proceeded out of the throne, as well as voices, and in the foreground were seven lamps of fire (see Revelation 4).

In God's right hand was a book, which was sealed on the backside with seven seals. It was not known what was in the book, but an angel soon appeared and asked if there was anyone worthy enough to loosen the seals and open it. No one answered at first, but finally one of the elders stepped forward and said that only "the lion of the tribe of Judah, the Root of David" (Revelation 5:5), could open it. It was Jehovah himself, in other words, a Lamb slain for the sins of the world, who now agreed to break the seals and open the book (see Revelation 5).

As Jehovah loosened the seals one by one, the first four portions of the book depicted horses: white, red, black, and pale in color respectively, each one with a rider. These would later be known in literature as the four horses of the apocalypse. A brief annotation accompanying each horse and rider referred to an era of human history, but these were vague and ambiguous. Not until the fifth seal was there something more substantive—a scene denoting the early Christian era and "the souls of them that were slain for the word of God, and for the testimony which they held" (Revelation 6:9).

Beginning with the sixth seal, the annotation was much more descriptive and told of a great earthquake that would take place in the future and a time when unusual phenomena would appear in the sky. The sun would be darkened, and the moon would become as blood. "And the stars of heaven fell unto the earth, even as a fig tree casteth her untimely figs, when she is shaken of a mighty wind. And the heaven departed as a scroll when it is rolled together; and every mountain and island were moved out of their places" (Revelation 6:13–14).

As the seventh and final seal was opened, "there was silence in heaven about the space of half an hour" (Revelation 8:1). At that time, there were seven angels standing before God in the temple, to whom were given seven trumpets, and the angels prepared themselves to sound them. Altogether, the account constitutes an impressive and unusual drama (see Revelation 8).

The scriptures imply that each period with its corresponding seal represents a time period of one thousand years. Although the Bible does not say so specifically, it seems to suggest that seven thousand years of history will pass on the earth from the time of Adam and Eve in the Garden of Eden to the end of the period of time known as the Millennium.

In these scriptures, the number seven has symbolic significance and is repeated many times. This scene from Revelation, for example, references the book with seven seals and notes that "there were seven lamps of fire burning before the throne, which are the seven Spirits of God" (Revelation 4:5). Morever, there were "the seven angels which stood before God, and to them were given seven trumpets" (Revelation 8:2).

Finally, in the 77th section of the Doctrine and Covenants, a book containing the revelations and religious commentaries of Joseph Smith, it confirms what the Bible suggests concerning the alleged periods of history represented by the seals. This section of scripture is the only one that offers any proof that what the Bible implies is correct. And while the Bible only suggests that seven thousand years will pass from the time of the Garden of Eden to the Millennium, the Doctrine and Covenants clearly identifies and explains this idea.

The Doctrine and Covenants was first published in 1835, and along with the Book of Mormon, which appeared five years earlier, the two records constitute the primary doctrine of the restored Church of Jesus Christ in the latter days. The intent of this additional scripture was not only to document the restoration of a church that existed in the meridian of time but also to supplement and substantiate the teachings of the Holy Bible, which were often being called into question or misinterpreted.

The Doctrine and Covenants has proved invaluable for confirming information that was once tentative or uncertain, including the question relating to the seven divisions of human history. For instance, it more fully explains what the sealed book contained: "We are to understand that it contains the revealed will, mysteries, and the works of God; the hidden things of his economy concerning this earth during the seven thousand years of its continuance, or its temporal existence" (D&C 77:6). And then, concerning the seals themselves, it says that "the first seal contains the things of the first thousand years, and the second also of the second thousand years, and so on until the seventh" (D&C 77:7).

At a time when there is no consensus as to how long mankind has lived upon the earth since the Garden of Eden or how much longer it will be until the end of the Millennium, the Doctrine and Covenants asserts categorically that it will be seven thousand years. In unmistakable language, it not only gives the duration of time from the days of Adam and Eve to the present, but it also describes what will happen immediately prior to the Lord's Second Coming. In a condensed scriptural dissertation, and in connection with the commonly accepted chronology of today's calendar, it tells explicitly what will occur at the beginning of the seventh millennium, which should be sometime during the twenty-first century!

Section 77 continues:

> We are to understand that as God made the world in six days, and on the seventh day he finished his work, and sanctified it, and also formed man out of the dust of the earth, even so, in the beginning of the seventh thousand years will the Lord God sanctify the earth, and complete the salvation of man, and judge all things, and shall redeem all things, except that which he hath not put into his power, when he shall have sealed all things, unto the end of all things; and the sounding of the trumpets of the seven angels are the preparing and finishing of his work, in the beginning of the seventh thousand years—the preparing of the way before the time of his coming. (D&C 77:12)

The Second Coming, therefore, will take place sometime in the *beginning* of the new millennium. This general term could mean that the final events before the start of the Millennium might happen over an extended period of time, even during the major part of the century. These events will then be followed by the First Resurrection and the final judgment and redemption, in addition to a burning and sanctification of the earth. But regardless of the exact time, everything will happen eventually, and the ending climax will occur very suddenly and unexpectedly!

Certainly, the scriptures in the Doctrine and Covenants are timely and informative and constitute a remarkable revelation. In them is a reliable report of when the Second Coming will take place and under what circumstances. The signal of the trumpets spoken of in the Book of Revelation will closely follow the opening of the seventh seal and will represent the preparation and completion of the Lord's work—"the preparing of the way before the time of his coming."

In regard to the accounts of the seals in the Doctrine and Covenants and the Book of Revelation, however, there appears to be a discrepancy in connection with the sixth seal. At least one of the four predicted events, and possibly all of them, is something definitely reserved for the seventh seal! This implies that during the formation of the Bible during ancient times, an error in translation and transmission occurred in which the actual sequence of events was altered. And although that is a serious and controversial assertion to make, it is true.

The most obvious error is where it says that the heavens will open as a scroll when it is rolled together—an event that obviously will occur during the time of the seventh seal. This is the exact time, in fact, when the face of the Lord will be revealed as he appears "in the clouds of heaven with power and great glory" (Matthew 24:30).

The misplacement of this final event implies that others listed in the sixth seal have also been placed in an inaccurate order, especially the passage pertaining to every mountain and island being moved out of their places. In addition, the great earthquake and the unusual phenomena relating to the sun, moon, and stars would consequently occur in the seventh seal as well.

What this amounts to, once again, is that a definite problem exists in the Book of Revelation relating to the contents of the sixth seal, all of which more accurately belong to the seventh seal that follows. As a consequence, the actual conditions of the sixth seal, referring to those things that will happen during the sixth period of a thousand years in the earth's history, might be listed as follows:

1. Widespread earthquakes
2. Wars and rumors of wars
3. Famines and pestilence
4. The preaching of the gospel throughout the world.

These events are cited in the 24th chapter of Matthew in the New Testament as characteristics of the last days. Moreover, major events such as Genghis Khan conquering Asia and killing more than five million people, the bubonic plague in the fourteenth century taking another twenty-four million, and the regime of Nazi Germany executing six million Jews during World War II are all the type of atrocity and pestilence that might be representative of things pertaining to the sixth seal.

Again, there are problems in Revelation, including chronological inconsistencies, which have not yet been solved. Their resolution appears unlikely for the time being, but in the meantime, with information gained from both ancient and modern scripture, a tentative but reasonable view of a very puzzling situation can still be obtained.

Finally, the "half hour" of silence in heaven mentioned after the seventh seal is opened is a mysterious period of time that cannot be definitively explained relative to a comparable duration of time on earth. According to 2 Peter 3:8, one day of God's time is equal to a thousand years on earth, making one half hour on the earth approximately twenty-one years. This would permit a considerable length of time for many things to take place in preparation for the Lord's Second Coming.

And yet there is an alternative interpretation of *silence* that presents another possibility. A period of "silence" is mentioned in connection with the time immediately following the Second Coming when the earth is to be burned with fire, and an idea in scripture sheds further light on what *silence* might mean. The account is found in Doctrine and Covenants: "For all flesh is corrupted before me," the Lord says, speaking to members of the newly organized church in the latter days, "and the powers of darkness prevail upon the earth, among the children of men, in the presence of all the hosts of heaven—Which causeth silence to reign, and all eternity is pained, and the angels are waiting the great command to reap down the earth, to gather the tares that they may be burned; and, behold, the enemy is combined" (38:11–12).

The use of the word *silence* in this instance is extremely meaningful in connection with an era of history where standards of human conduct and morality have reached an all-time low. There is no question that intellectual advancement, including science and technology, have reached an unprecedented high while things of a spiritual nature have often regressed. In today's world, it is easy to believe that darkness prevails upon the earth and all eternity is pained. As a consequence, "angels are waiting the great command to reap down the earth."

It is possible, then, that the seventh seal has already been opened and that the Second Coming is imminent. The period of silence, whatever the duration of time might be, has very likely already begun, and events and circumstances in the world today are preparatory to when the Lord will come a second time. Never during modern history has there been a more appropriate time for this to happen!

The massive burning that will take place upon the earth's surface soon after the Lord's return is especially significant. Sometime following the morning of the First Resurrection, a devastating holocaust will occur in which fire will spread throughout the world, consuming every corrupted thing in its path. Like a giant tidal wave of flame or a raging cyclone, it will cleanse the earth with fire—much like it was cleansed with water during the great flood of Noah's time. The declaration that angels are waiting for the signal to commence this work definitely adds to the urgency of the situation.

It is not pleasant to visualize the fiery destruction that will take place in the future, a destruction which, in the words of the prophet Malachi, will "burn as an oven; and all the proud, yea and all that do wickedly, shall be as stubble" (Malachi 4:1). Every impure substance upon the earth that is in need of cleansing will be consumed in preparation for the planet's coming renewal and paradisiacal glory. The time it will take to accomplish this is unknown. It could be gradual or sudden. But when it is over, the

37

earth will be relieved of the telestial condition it has had for over six thousand years, and it will be given terrestrial status.

After six thousand years, the earth will return to the condition that existed during the time of Adam and Eve in the Garden of Eden. And if the earth itself could speak, it would undoubtedly express relief from the wear and tear it has received from the long centuries of human habitation and from the disrespect and mistreatment that people in all different time periods have given it. On that occasion, it will be extremely weary, not only because of peoples' neglect in caring for the environment but, in a religious sense, because of their wickedness and waywardness. Moreover, if it had the power of speech, the earth would very likely express the need for a well-deserved rest, something alluded to in a verse of modern scripture where the earth takes on the voice of Mother Earth, or Nature: "Wo, wo is me; the mother of men. I am pained, I am weary, because of the wickedness of my children. When shall I rest, and be cleansed from the filthiness which is gone forth out of me? When will my Creator sanctify me, that I may rest, and righteousness for a season abide upon my face?" (Moses 7:48).

All of this provides an interesting commentary to what will happen in the future after the earth has passed through six time periods into the seventh seal and a baptism of fire has engulfed and covered its surface. It also calls attention to an unusual aspect of the earth itself, namely the fact that it is much more than just a planet in space revolving in orbit with other planets around the sun. It is not merely a conventional sphere, consisting of crust, mantle, and inner and outer cores, but rather an actual living entity, analogous in some ways to a human being and going through some of the same stages of existence, particularly those pertaining to religion and spirituality!

7

EARTH AS A LIVING BEING

I n the beginning, God created the heaven and the earth. And
the earth was without form, and void; and darkness was upon
the face of the deep. And the Spirit of God moved upon the face
of the waters" (Genesis 1:1–2). Such was the birth of the earth—a
solitary planet in space that at first appeared to have no more
than just an ordinary beginning. And yet this was an orb that
had a remarkable destiny and would someday be the birthplace
of a God. Out of all the planets that had been created, this was
the one selected for the birth of Jehovah, the son of Elohim and
of the mortal virgin Mary.

On the occasion of the earth's birth, the planet was apparently
a solid sphere under whose surface flowed vast areas of subterranean water. In Noah's time, these waters rose and completely
submerging the earth. According to scripture, it was during this
time that "the Spirit of God moved upon the face of the waters."

In the Book of Psalms, there is an interesting comment associating the creation of the earth with subterranean water. A single
verse recorded in Psalm 24:2, for example, as it is translated in
the New English Bible, states, "For it was he who founded it upon
the seas and planted it firm upon the waters beneath." The King
James Version gives a similar account of the same verse: "For

he hath founded it upon the seas, and established it upon the floods."

Robert Davidson, who was once an instructor in Old Testament Language and Literature at the University of Glasgow, gives the following commentary on the probability of subterranean water emerging to the earth's surface in the form of seas: "From other Old Testament passages," he writes, "it is clear that the earth is regarded as a solid disk founded upon the subterranean waters which surface in the seas."[1]

Also, there is the biblical account that describes what happened on the fourth day of creation:

> And God said, Let there be lights in the firmament of the heaven to divide the day from the night; and let them be for signs, and for seasons, and for days, and years:
>
> And let them be for lights in the firmament of the heaven to give light upon the earth: and it was so.
>
> And God made two great lights; the greater light to rule the day, and the lesser light to rule the night: he made the stars also.
>
> And God set them in the firmament of the heaven to give light upon the earth,
>
> And to rule over the day, and over the night, and to divide the light from the darkness: and God saw that it was good. (Genesis 1:14–18)

It is reasonable to think that the sun, moon, and stars were not brought to the vicinity of the earth and placed in the firmament, but rather that the earth was brought to the lights in the sky. One possibility, therefore, is that the planet earth was taken from an orbit in a former location and moved to its present orbit around the sun. In any case, it is an interesting observation.

It is also important to note that the earth possessed a spiritual nature, as well as one that was temporal or physical. As the spirit and body of an individual constitute the soul of man, so might the combined spiritual and temporal parts of the planet be regarded as the soul of the earth. This implies that as a human being is much more than heart, lungs, and a myriad of parts, so also is the earth much more than just crust, mantle and the inner cores.

This idea is further illustrated by what eventually happened in the Garden of Eden. When Adam transgressed the law, as recorded in the biblical account, it was not only he that fell but also the earth. The earth was cursed for Adam's sake and changed from an immortal to a mortal condition. Like humanity, however, the planet was not lost. Through the atonement of Jesus Christ, it was also redeemed from the Fall and is now successfully filling the measure of its creation.

This means that the earth, following its birth or creation, eventually entered a mortal existence that included a type of probation. And during the last several thousand years of time, it has been going through certain stages that are comparable to those that a human being experiences.

The earth, therefore, is subject to the basic religious ordinances of being born of the water and of the Spirit as outlined in the Bible. Its baptism by water occurred at the time of the great Flood in the days of Noah, and the fiery baptism of the Spirit will take place at the end of the world, shortly after the Second Coming and at the beginning of the Millennium. It is then that the earth will be renewed and restored to its former glory.

After the earth's spiritual baptism, another thousand years of history will come. That final thousand years will be followed by the eventual death, quickening, and resurrection of the earth. This will complete the process for it to obtain its own salvation and exaltation.

Such an unusual view of the earth, noting its progression from birth to resurrection, is both unorthodox and revolutionary and is the result of modern scripture. And although it is a religious view that not everyone readily understands and accepts, it is true.

The concept also complements the idea that the planet earth is, once again, not just another orb in the sky. It is one that has a very unusual destiny, having been the birthplace of Jehovah and the site of his personal ministries—not only in Palestine but in other regions of the earth as well. From the very beginning, it has had an unusual role among the planets. It has very likely been brought from another part of the galaxy or universe, and it might possibly return one day to its original location where it will become a celestial abode, occupying a location in space near the throne of God himself!

Notes

1. Robert Davidson, *The Cambridge Bible Commentary, Genesis 1–11* (London: Cambridge University Press), 20.

8

THE DOCTRINE AND COVENANTS

The Doctrine and Covenants is an extremely important book that contains the revelations and religious commentaries of the early years of the Church. It is highly significant because it exists at a time when scholars cannot agree on how long mankind has lived upon the earth or when certain events and phenomena took place during the time of the Old Testament, particularly those events that occurred prior to the first millennium before Christ.

It is also uncertain how many years the time periods mentioned in the Bible contained, such as the life spans of the ancient prophets and patriarchs. Consequently, it is difficult to synchronize things that happened in the Bible with corresponding secular accounts and to reconcile the chronological differences.

Of particular importance in this regard is information found in modern scripture. The Doctrine and Covenants declares that the earth's human history up to the present time consists of six one-thousand-year periods. This fact establishes the time of Adam and Eve in the Garden of Eden at about 4,000 years before Christ—a date similar to the chronology in the King James Version of the Bible (see D&C 77:6–7). Amid contemporary controversy, this revelation is extremely significant. It defines a frame of reference relating to the human experience that had been introduced almost two hundred years previously but was never confirmed until the time of Joseph Smith.

During the years 1650 to 1654, for example, an archbishop named James Ussher, who was an Anglican prelate of Ireland, published a chronology of the Old Testament that he had made using the Hebrew text of the Bible as the basis of his research. Among his conclusions at the time was the declaration that the creation of the earth took place approximately four thousand years before the birth of Jesus Christ.

Ussher's chronology was logical and systematic. It divided human history into several meaningful periods. The first two thousand years covered the time from Adam to Abraham. That was followed by another two thousand years that led to the time of Christ. Two thousand years following Christ then led up to the end of the sixth millennium. Scholars and the general public accepted this system for more than two centuries, and it was included in the King James Bible as marginal dates and footnotes.

But during the nineteenth century, the computations created by Ussher began to lose credibility, and today his chronology is seldom used. The dates in his chronology do not always synchronize with events in secular history. It is ironic, therefore, after all of this time, that a new scripture should suddenly appear in the time of Joseph Smith that reinforced Ussher's chronology. This new scripture refers to the unusual record in the book of Revelation that was sealed on the back with seven seals. Concerning the contents of this book, Doctrine and Covenants 77 gives the following information: "We are to understand," the scripture says, "that it contains the revealed will, mysteries, and works of God; the hidden things of his economy concerning this earth *during the seven thousand years of its continuance, or its temporal existence*" (D&C 77:6; emphasis added).

The Doctrine and Covenants explicitly divulges the extent of the world's entire human history from the very beginning in the

Garden of Eden to the end of the biblical Millennium. It remarkably confirms how many years have been involved so far in the earth's "continuance or its temporal existence," which refers to the first six thousand years. And regardless of what public reaction might be to this kind of information, in view of its abruptness, conciseness, and brevity, as well as its bold assertion, it stands as a revolutionary statement that God revealed through a modern prophet.

This one statement, if accepted as truth, completely alters the thinking within current dating systems pertaining to the Old Testament and again gives credibility to the computations of James Ussher. At the same time, it implies that certain adjustments in both secular and biblical records will eventually be made to reconcile chronological differences. This could result in adjusting secular history to fit prophecy at times, rather than vice versa.

The Doctrine and Covenants also includes an extremely important statement concerning the opening of the seven seals. Regarding this event, modern scripture correlates the seventh day of the earth's creation with the seventh thousand years of its temporal existence and tells specifically what will happen at the beginning of that final period:

> We are to understand that as God made the world in six days, and on the seventh day he finished his work, and sanctified it, and also formed man out of the dust of the earth, even so, in the beginning of the seventh thousand years will the Lord God sanctify the earth, and complete the salvation of man, and judge all things, and shall redeem all things, except that which he hath not put into his power, when he shall have sealed all things, unto the end of all things; and the sounding of the trumpets of the seven angels [is] the preparing and finishing of his work, in the beginning of the seventh thousand years—*the preparing of the way before the time of his coming.* (D&C 77:12; emphasis added)

In the commencement of the seventh millennium, therefore, events of tremendous importance will occur, including the burning and sanctification of the earth and the processes of final judgment and redemption. All things relating to the previous six thousand years will be brought to a close. But the remarkable revelation given in Section 77 gives one more thing: an announcement of the Second Coming of Jesus Christ and the occurrences preceding his return. The sounding trumpets of the seven angels recorded in the book of Revelation, in other words, dramatically describe the final preparations that will occur during the beginning of the seventh millennium, after which the Second Coming and the biblical Millennium will take place.

This preparation could come at a variety of times, of course. The only definite thing is that the "preparing and finishing" of the Lord's work "before the time of his coming" will happen sometime in the beginning of the seventh thousand years. This means that it could perhaps be anywhere from 2010 to 2050, or even a period well beyond that time. Scripture and current revelation do not give a specific time, and no other sources of information on the topic exist. This uncertainty is also a reminder of the words Jesus said to his disciples on one occasion during his earthly ministry, which today still come ringing down from the past: "But of that day and hour knoweth no man," he said, referring to the end of the world, "no, not the angels of heaven, but my Father only" (Matthew 24:36).

9

A QUADRANGLE OF EVENTS

As the Second Coming draws closer, four momentous events are scheduled to take place. These will be preceded by an untold number of natural disasters and cataclysmic disturbances. Hardly a month or a year goes by during modern times without an earthquake, tidal wave, destructive flood, fire, or meteorological disturbance being reported. These natural disasters are noticeably and statistically on the increase. Unfortunately, they create a background for the quadrangle of events that will inevitably occur.

The first and second of these events will be the dramatic construction of two temples—one in the eastern part of the world and the other in the west. These temples will not necessarily be extraordinary buildings in appearance or size, but their introduction to the world scene will be highly significant and noteworthy because of what they represent. In light of what has happened in the past, as well as in religious prophecy, these structures will reveal the impending urgency and imminence of the Second Coming.

In the western part of the state of Missouri, the church restored through the instrumentality of Joseph Smith almost two hundred years ago is planning to build a large temple complex and city in an area designated as Zion, a namesake and counter-part of the place associated with the patriarch Enoch in the Old Testament. During the same general time period, the Church will also reconstruct a temple in Jerusalem in the vicinity where one existed in the time of Jesus. These two structures and the two cities in which they are located will be designated by the latter-day Church as religious world capitals—one in the western part of the world as well as one in the eastern.

The building of the temple in what has been called the "center place of Zion," will be a continuation of a vast program of temple construction already in progress, albeit on a different scale. The temple in Zion, in fact, will not be just one building but twenty-four, according to the original plan. It will be a combination of individual temples occupying two large city blocks of fifteen acres each. These twenty-four temples have also been described as rooms all joined together in a circular form and arched over the center,[1] but the original plan appears to include separate structures. According to a plan created by Joseph Smith, who was the original designer and architect of the temple complex, there were to be twelve temples on each block, situated alternately in rows of three. The first of these buildings, which would be eighty-seven feet long and sixty-one feet wide, was to be built near the center of the first block.[2]

In any case, the preliminary plan has been in existence for well over one hundred and fifty years, and when the time comes for its implementation, the actual construction of the temple complex and the central portion of the city of Zion and its environs could occur very quickly.

What is important in all of this, of course, is that this particular temple, the construction of which will be a tremendous undertaking, is scheduled to take place *before* the time of the Second Coming. Joseph Smith implied this when he said that a temple of similar standing would definitely be built in Jerusalem during this time period. "Judah must return," he said, referring to the gathering of the Jewish people in modern-day Palestine. "Jerusalem must be rebuilt, and the temple, and water come out from under the temple . . . and all of this must be done before the Son of Man will make his appearance."[3] Both temples, the one in Palestine and the other in America, will be in place at the time of Christ's return.

One surprising revelation about the temple that will be built in America is that the practice of animal sacrifice will be restored at that time. This practice, which has been dormant in Christianity since Christ's resurrection, will temporarily be reintroduced as part of a "restitution of all things" during an era in the latter days termed scripturally as the Dispensation of the Fulness of Times. The concept behind this practice is not always easy to understand, particularly in the context of modern society, yet it was a principle Joseph Smith fully comprehended. One thing he emphasized was that after animal sacrifice has been restored, people will continue to practice it until the Second Coming of Christ. During the intervening period, it will continue "from generation to generation." For whatever reason, this ancient principal will be extended for an indefinite period of time "with all its authority, power, and blessings."[4] All of this is not only interesting and significant, but it also confirms the existence of a temple in the city of Zion (also called the New Jerusalem) prior to the Millennium and is one of the major signs of the times and the final stages of the latter days.

Another event of great importance will be the construction or so-called reconstruction of the ancient temple in the city of Jerusalem. Among all the signs that will be given, this is one of the most interesting, yet possibly one of the most difficult to fulfill as far as human participation is concerned. But it is an event that needs to occur *before* the time of the Second Coming.

After the temple built by Solomon was destroyed, Zerubbabel and his associates rebuilt it on the same site following the Babylonian Captivity. This second temple stood for approximately five hundred years, going through many different stages and desecrations.

Finally, a short time before the birth of Christ, Herod the Great began making changes and improvements. He enlarged and refurbished the previous structure at an enormous financial cost and turned it into something far beyond anything previously known. Though Herod himself was a despicable ruler, Jesus accepted the new temple as his own during his earthly ministry, referring to it on one occasion as his Father's house.

Three different temples, therefore, once existed at the location in Jerusalem regarded today as the Temple Mount. All three have since been destroyed, but in their place is a memory held by millions of people throughout the world belonging to the religions of Islam, Judaism, and Christianity. They all look upon the Holy City as part of their religious heritage. Certain members of two of these groups, in fact, say that someday they want to rebuild the ancient temple. The restored latter-day church, a Jewish organization called the Temple Institute, and possibly others look upon this as an important undertaking and a specific goal for the future.

However, Jews or Christians trying to build a temple on the Temple Mount would pose a real problem. In the mind of Islam, this particular location is the third most important religious site in the world, the other two being Mecca and Medina. Anyone threatening or disrupting the status of the Dome of the Rock or the nearby al-Aqsa Mosque (both located on the Temple Mount) would spark open warfare, a potentiality that already exists between the Israelis and Palestinians.

A proposal to construct a temple on the Temple Mount, however, in the exact spot where the original temple stood might still be a possibility. If the theory of Asher Kaufman, a professor associated with the Hebrew University in Jerusalem, is correct, the location of the earlier temple was not on the site of the Dome of the Rock, as commonly believed, but some twenty-six meters to the north. This would allow a new temple to be built on the same location as the original by either Jews or Christians without seriously disrupting any religious worship of the Muslims. And even if all of these calculations should prove to be incorrect, a new temple might ultimately be constructed at some other place in the city.

The latter-day Church, for example, could possibly build a temple at a site near the Mount of Olives. The Church has already erected an imposing building in that area for educational purposes, and it is not unlikely that someday the Church could build a temple there. But wherever such a temple is constructed, and whoever it is that builds it, the event will be fraught with meaning and significance. Not only will it be a memorable religious occurrence, in and of itself, but it will also be an important sign of the times.

In the meantime, there will be a third occurrence in the quadrangle of events before the Second Coming, at a time when Jesus, or Jehovah, will make an appearance in Adam-ondi-Ahman. This place is unknown to most people in today's society, but it is one of great importance. In this quiet valley in northwestern Missouri, Christ is scheduled to make a historic visit. It will be reminiscent of another visit that occurred in this same vicinity more than 5,000 years ago:

> Three years previous to the death of Adam, he called Seth, Enos, Cainan, Mahalaleel, Jared, Enoch, and Methuselah, who were all high priests, with the residue of his posterity who were righteous, into the valley of Adam-ondi-Ahman, and there bestowed upon them his last blessing. And the Lord appeared unto them, and they rose up and blessed Adam, and called him Michael, the prince, the archangel.
>
> And the Lord administered comfort unto Adam, and said unto him: I have set thee to be at the head; a multitude of nations shall come of thee, and thou art a prince over them forever. And Adam stood up in the midst of the congregation; and notwithstanding he was bowed down with age, being full of the Holy Ghost, predicted whatsoever should befall his posterity unto the latest generation. (D&C 107:55–56)

51

This was a momentous occasion that took place somewhere outside the Garden of Eden almost one thousand years after the expulsion of Adam and Eve. The event did not occur in the Old World, as most people believe, but rather in the New World. The belief compatible in the Doctrine and Covenants, for example, is that the site of the garden mentioned in the book of Genesis was in present-day North America and not on the other side of the globe in Mesopotamia or some other locale.

Another important fact that modern scripture has further revealed is that the Garden of Eden was not only in North America but was specifically in what is now northwestern Missouri. Along with additional information found in the Bible, this record describes events in historic meetings yet to come. In the book of Daniel, for example, the prophet had a vision that told about someone called the Ancient of Days, who was Adam, who would come for the purpose of reviewing and judging the people. Undoubtedly this was a future occurrence, yet how much of it pertains to what will occur at Adam-ondi-Ahman in western Missouri is unclear. In any case, the principal figure involved is Adam. Daniel wrote, "I beheld till the thrones were cast down, and the Ancient of Days did sit, whose garment was white as snow, and the hair of his head like the pure wool: his throne was like a fiery flame, and his wheels as burning fire. A fiery stream issued and came forth from before him: thousand thousands ministered unto him, and ten thousand times ten thousand stood before him: the judgment was set, and the books were opened" (Daniel 7:9–10).

In this dream, Daniel beheld Adam, appearing in white, with the bearing and majesty of a prince or king. Throngs of people attended him, according to the dream's description, even to the extent of one hundred million. At that time, the books were opened, and Adam assumed his position before the people as magistrate and judge.

The next section of the dream, however, presents a very different scene: "I saw in the night visions, and, behold, one like the Son of man came with the clouds of heaven, and came to the Ancient of days, and they brought him near before him. And there was given him dominion, and glory, and a kingdom, that all people, nations, and languages, should serve him: his dominion is an everlasting dominion, which shall not pass away, and his kingdom that which shall not be destroyed" (Daniel 7:13–14).

At this point, Daniel's dream appears to be divided into two separate occurrences—one showing Adam in a judicial capacity, the other showing the Son of man, meaning Jehovah or Jesus Christ, visiting Adam. In one, there are countless millions of people, but in the other, there is a much smaller number.

When Joseph Smith commented on this second occurrence, he said nothing about any judgments that would take place, but he spoke instead of power and dominion and the transfer of authority. "Daniel in his seventh chapter speaks of the Ancient of days," Joseph explained. "He means the oldest man, our father Adam, Michael; he will call his children together and hold a council with them to prepare them for the coming of the Son of Man. He [Adam] is the father of the human family, and presides over the spirits of all men, and all that have had the keys must stand before him in this grand council . . . Adam delivers up his stewardship to Christ, that which was delivered to him as holding the keys of the universe, but retains his standing as head of the human family."[5]

Again, there is no mention of any books being opened or any judgment being conducted. The main reason for holding this second meeting at Adam-ondi-Ahman will be to conduct a council in which to prepare "for the coming of the Son of Man." Certain things need to be done ahead of time, however, including people making reports to Adam and delivering up stewardships or assignments of responsibility. Adam in turn will then deliver his own stewardship to Christ. It will be a grand and noble operation according to the order of the priesthood that will officially place the keys of administration and leadership in the hands of one individual. All of these things are needed for the time of the Second Coming.

Indeed, the things which Daniel saw in his dream were extraordinary and of monumental importance, and they left him bewildered and with many questions. "I Daniel was grieved in my spirit in the midst of my body," he said, "and the visions of my head troubled me. . . . my cogitations much troubled me, and my countenance changed in me: but I kept the matter in my heart" (Daniel 7:15, 28).

Surely the event in Adam-ondi-Ahman will be a momentous occasion, and it is an occurrence to anticipate. But one important question remains concerning the number of people that will be there. How many will be eligible and invited to attend? Because of what is depicted in the first part of Daniel's dream, some are of the opinion that a hundred million people or more will be in attendance. Yet anyone who has been in the valley of Adam-ondi-Ahman and walked through it will undoubtedly agree that the area would not accommodate that many people (a number comparable to one third of the United States's population). Even if areas several miles away might be considered a part of Adam-ondi-Ahman, the number of one hundred million is still too overwhelming.

The more likely and logical explanation is that the predicted gathering and meeting in this particular valley will be a secret and unobserved event. A relatively small number of people will be there, compared to the general population, and yet at the same time those in attendance will be regarded as a huge multitude, all invited by appointment. It will be similar to a priesthood meeting or solemn assembly. All those in past dispensations of the gospel who have possessed the highest and most important keys pertaining to the priesthood will be there to make reports and deliver up stewardships. Without question, it will be a very private affair, albeit a very large one, and it will come and go secretly "as a thief in the night" (Thessalonians 5:2).

To those in attendance, it will be a signal that the Lord's second advent is imminent, that everything is on schedule, and that important occurrences lie just ahead. One of these, for example, will be another appearance by Jesus Christ—the fourth event of the quadrangle. And although it is uncertain exactly when this will occur, it is very possible it will occur in the central part of the United States soon after the temple complex is completed in the city of Zion.

An account of this event is found in the book of Revelation in the Bible immediately following the account of the opening of the sixth seal. In connection with other events in this area of scripture, the event in question might apply to the opening of the seventh seal instead of the sixth. The scripture tells about four angels standing together on the four corners of the earth, holding the four winds in their hands. Another angel, possessing the seal of the living God, eventually appears, ascending from the east and crying out in a loud voice to the four angels. "Hurt not the earth," he says, "neither the sea, nor the trees, till we have sealed the servants of our God in their foreheads. And I heard the number of them which were sealed," quoting the one recording the scripture, "and there were sealed an hundred and forty and four thousand of all the tribes of the children of Israel . . . .

"And I looked, and lo, a Lamb stood on the mount Sion, and with him an hundred and forty and four thousand, having his Father's name written in their foreheads. And I heard a voice from heaven, as the voice of many waters, and as the voice of a great thunder: and I heard the voice of harpers harping with their harps. And they sang as it were a new song before the throne . . . and no man could learn that song but the hundred and forty and four thousand, which were redeemed from the earth" (Revelation 7:3–4; 14:13).

This particular scripture, much like others in the Bible, has been the subject of opinion and controversy. Although the biblical account lists the names of the tribes involved (all except the tribe of Dan), it says nothing about the meaning of the sealing taking place. The Doctrine and Covenants, however, provides a possible answer.

"We are to understand," the scripture says, "that those who are sealed are high priests, ordained unto the holy order of God, to administer the everlasting gospel; for they are they who are ordained out of every nation, kindred, tongue, and people, by the angels to whom is given power over the nations of the earth, to bring as many as will come to the church of the Firstborn" (D&C 77:11).

The reference to the "church of the Firstborn" is a clue to the meaning and chronology of the "sealing" of one hundred and forty-four thousand people. These high priests, as they are called, will be missionaries that will proclaim the gospel throughout the world—an event taking place before the Second Coming, as Matthew 24:14 implies. The church of the Firstborn, according to Doctrine the and Covenants, is a term synonymous with the highest level of heaven, or the celestial kingdom (see D&C 76:57, 70).

Following this important quadrangle of events, it will only be a short time before a final countdown of events will take place, the first of which will be the return of the lost tribes of Israel. These are people who have been lost from the knowledge of modern society for ages, some of whom will possibly be part of the missionary force of the one hundred and forty-four thousand. Certainly their future reappearance will be miraculous and supernatural and will be one of the final signs that the seventh thousand years of the earth's temporal existence are well under way and that the earth will soon be plagued with a series of catastrophic devastations.

Notes

1. N. B. Lundwall (ed.), *Temples of the Most High* (Salt Lake City: Bookcraft), 218.

2. Joseph Smith, *History of the Church of Jesus Christ of Latter-day Saints,* vol. 1. (Salt Lake City: Deseret Book), 357–360.

3. Ibid., vol. 5. 337.

4. Ibid., vol. 4. 211–212.

5. Ibid., vol. 3. 386–387.

10

THE FINAL
COUNTDOWN

No one knows for certain the order and sequence of the concluding events prior to the Second Coming, and the following list is only tentative and theoretical. But the main occurrences are in place, some of which are miraculous and almost unbelievable and form an impressive prelude to what is about to happen. The countdown of events begins at number seven, possibly the most significant and symbolic number in the annals of scripture.

7. Following centuries of isolation at a remote location, the lost tribes of Israel will finally return in an extraordinary manner.

6. The Battle of Armageddon, a final conflict prophesied in the book of Revelation, will take place in the area of Jerusalem and the Valley of Esdraelon or Jezreel.

5. A gigantic earthquake, a type heretofore unknown, will occur along with other quakes, breaking down the mountains and shaking the nations.

4. In a wide sweep of transformation, the lands of Jerusalem and Zion are "turned back into their own place," and the earth's surface is radically changed.

3. Phenomena relating to the sun, moon, and stars take place in the sky, and eventually the sign of the Son of man is revealed.

2. The waters of the great deep, involving all of the seas and oceans, are "driven back into the north countries."

1. As a concluding event, the "curtain of heaven" is unfolded, and the face of the Lord is unveiled.

At this point, the Second Coming and what has been called the morning and afternoon of the first resurrection will occur. Then sometime during this same time period, a worldwide burning of the earth will take place, followed by the commencement of the Millennium. Surely the confluence of so many important events in what has been referred to as the end of the world is almost beyond comprehension, but it will all happen, and everything that has been predicted will eventually occur!

11

DRAMA OF RESTORATION AND CONFLICT

One of the creeds or articles of faith that Joseph Smith expounded in the latter-day church, which he through the ministering of angels had been commanded to restore, reads as follows: "We believe in the literal gathering of Israel and in the restoration of the ten tribes" (Article of Faith 10).

In a modern day, when reference to ten tribes is probably unfamiliar to most people, especially in a traditional sense saying they are lost, it might be surprising that such would be part of a religious creed. Yet soon after the newly-organized church began baptizing people and forming congregations, an angel appeared in a temple that had recently been built in Kirtland, Ohio, and restored "the keys of the gathering of Israel from the four parts of the earth, and the leading of the ten tribes from the land of the north" (D&C 110:11).

This was an event that brought to the forefront of contemporary society a subject and idea that had been absent for centuries. It told of the affairs of the House of Israel, dating back as an earthly institution to the time of Abraham, Isaac, and Jacob, and was divided and dispersed during the eighth and sixth centuries B.C. when the people involved were conquered by invading armies. Since most of that time, any reference to the name of Israel, especially following the ministry of Jesus Christ, has generally been non-existent. Yet through the instrumentality of Joseph Smith it again became known.

Jacob, whose name was changed to Israel, had twelve sons during his lifetime, each of whom became the head of a tribe who together were regarded as the twelve tribes or House of Israel. In no place in Hebrew or Israelite history is there mention of a more prestigious organization, their entity as a people being first established as far back as pre-mortality.

In a society pertaining to earth, they became well known as slaves under the Egyptian pharaohs and were eventually led by Moses to a promised land in Palestine where they developed into a large population. Under the administration of their first three kings—Saul, David, and Solomon—they became a significant nation in the Middle East. In the year 930 B.C., however, the people were beset by political and economic differences and divided into two groups, one called the Kingdom of Judah and the other the Kingdom of Israel.

The first kingdom comprised the tribe of Judah and approximately one-half of the tribe of Benjamin, and a man named Rehoboam, son of Solomon, was king. The second retained the name of Israel and was led by a man called Jeroboam, the tribes involved being Reuben, Simeon, Dan, Naphtali, Gad, Asher, Issachar, Zebulun, and the other half of Benjamin. Joseph was not listed as a regular tribe but was represented by his two sons Ephraim and Manasseh. These were then regarded as the TEN TRIBES.

The tribe of Levi was also part of this group but was not recognized in the same way as the others because of its religious responsibilities. It eventually transferred to the Kingdom of Judah.

The two kingdoms existed separately until 721 B.C., at which time Israel was conquered by Assyria coming the north and disappeared as an independent nation in the Middle East. The same happened to Judah over a century later when it was overcome by the Chaldeans of Babylonia. In both cases thousands of the inhabitants were removed and taken into captivity.

In regard to the people known as the ten tribes, it is a common belief that most of them were deported as prisoners and were eventually scattered and dispersed among the nations. And yet apparently this was not the case. It was the Assyrian policy during this time period not to deport the entire population of a conquered city or region but rather only one-half or less. The other portion was left in the original area to mix with incoming colonists brought in from other parts of the Assyrian Empire.

Those who remained in their homeland, therefore, were the ones who later disseminated among the various countries. But the prisoners who were taken into captivity constitute an entirely different group, being deported northward to areas in Mesopotamia and eastward to the so-called cities of the Medes. A certain amount of these people also might have been dispersed further abroad, but at least some eventually banded together and traveled to the north where they became lost to the knowledge of society and since then have been known as the lost tribes of Israel.

The only account telling what took place on this occasion is found in the Apocrypha, a set of uncanonical scripture not recorded in the Old Testament. It describes the people's departure from Assyrian captivity as well as their journey into the north country.

"But they formed this plan for them selves," the record states, "that they would leave the multitude of the nations and go to a more distant region, where mankind had never lived, that there at least they might keep their statutes which they had not kept in their own land.

"And they went in by the narrow passages if the Euphrates River. For at that time the Most High performed signs for them, and stopped the channels of the river until they had passed over. Through that region there was a long way to go, a journey of a year and a half; and that country is called Arzareth."[1]

The Doctrine and Covenants gives the following explanation concerning the reliability and authenticity of the Apocrypha: "There are many things contained therein that are true, and it is mostly translated correctly; there are many things contained therein that are not true, which are the interpolations by the hands of men" (D&C 91:2).

Since the statements in question generally appear to be historical, rather than mystical or apocalyptic, they might well be in the category of those that are true. In any case, they form the only description of the tribes' departure, although in modern scripture, they are recognized as being in existence at an unknown location and will someday return in a miraculous manner.

The apocryphal references to "Arzareth," which in Hebrew means another land, and "the narrow passages of the Euphrates River" are the only clues as to where the ten tribes went. One thing appears certain, however, and that is that their general direction of travel was toward the north, far enough that they could escape from the multitude of the nations and find a more distant region where people had never gone before.

Where they might be today has always been a mystery, and yet in the description of the tribe's return, there is an implication that God will perform signs for them as he did when they crossed the narrow passages of the Euphrates River many centuries ago. At a time in the future, according to a description in the Doctrine and Covenants, prophets leading these people will smite the rocks, causing earth to give way and creating an avalanche of ice in front of them. A highway or pathway will then be raised up providing a final exit across an expanse of water.

"And they who are in the north countries shall come in remembrance before the Lord," the record says, "and their prophets shall hear his voice and shall no longer stay themselves; and they shall smite the rocks, and the ice shall flow down at their presence. And an highway shall be cast up in the midst of the great deep" (D&C 133:26–27).

Wherever the lost tribes might be, which obviously is not on any observable area of the earth, the conditions and circumstances of their dramatic reappearance will necessarily be miraculous, and even supernatural. This is despite the fact that people often resort to symbolism and figurative language in describing how the tribes will return. An example of this is a remark by a well-known scientist and church leader while talking to a congregation of the church that had been restored in the latter days. The speaker was James E. Talmage.

"There is a tendency among men," he said, "to explain away what they do not wish to understand in literal simplicity, and we as Latter-day Saints are not entirely free from the taint of that tendency." At the time, he was discussing the lost tribes, referring specifically to the prediction that someday they will return in an unusual manner.

"Some people say that prediction is to be explained in this way," he continued. "A gathering is in progress, and has been in progress from the early days of this church, and thus the 'lost tribes' are now being gathered but that we are not to look for the return of any body of people now unknown as to their whereabouts.

"True, the gathering is in progress," he concluded. "This is a gathering dispensation. But the prophecy stands that the tribes shall be brought forth from their hiding place, bringing their scriptures with them."[2]

Reference to a hiding place was unusual, and yet explicit, and correctly described the circumstances concerning the lost tribes and where they are presently located. It was a statement referring not only to their present circumstances but also to their return. Somewhere in the confines of the earth, therefore, at a place traditionally associated with the land of the north, the lost tribes of Israel exist as a nation. They are not intermingled with the different countries of the world, as some might suppose, but are living as a separate group of people at an undisclosed location.

Unlike in times past, little is said about them anymore, and on occasion when the subject of their return is mentioned, it is regarded almost as fiction. Yet in the future when the rumor comes that crumbling rock and ice have opened up a passageway in the north countries and a mysterious highway has appeared, people will then know that the ten tribes are finally on their way!

Joseph Smith, in his role of restoring the latter-day church, was definitely aware of many of these things, as well as the adverse conditions in the United States when future events would occur. His vision of things to come contained unfortunate, yet apparently necessary, circumstances preparatory to the return of the lost tribes. On one occasion he made a dramatic comment relative to their reappearance and restoration.

"And now I am prepared to say," he said, "by the authority of Jesus Christ, that not many years shall pass away before the United States shall present such a scene of bloodshed as has not a parallel in the history of our nation; pestilence, hail, famine, and earthquake will sweep the wicked of this generation from off the face of the land, to open and prepare the way for the return of the lost tribes of Israel from the north country."[3]

It was a dire forecast as to what will happen in America, but in view of all that has happened in the world today, it will be no more than what has been predicted for more distant places. Much more serious, in fact, is what will take place someday in the Middle East, in the vicinity of Jerusalem and Palestine. In a historic locality where adverse conditions have existed for centuries, and men and armies have fought on open battlefields, a final conflict will occur before the Second Coming originating in the Valley of Jezreel and Plain of Esdraelon in northern Palestine, also known as the Valley of Armageddon.

Very close in time to the return of the lost tribes, either before or after, this particular battle will be part of a grand culmination of events during the world's regular history. Following all of the wars that have been fought down through the centuries, this will be the last one before the world finally comes to an end. Again it is in this same general time period that the Second Coming will occur and the earth will be renewed and restored to a paradisia-cal glory.

In comparison with other wars, the Battle of Armageddon will in many ways be the worst conflict the world has ever seen. Although the weaponry and means of warfare might not always be highly sophisticated, the intensity of fighting will be unparal-leled. In the words of the prophet Joel, "There hath not been ever the like, neither shall be any more after it, even to the years of many generations" (Joel 2:2).

At the time of this great battle, the forces of Gog will come down from the north country out of the land called Magog, which traditionally is the same as ancient Scythia near the upper parts of the Black and Caspian Seas. In a modern world known for its high technology and scientific achievement, many of the invaders will appear as in days of old, "all of them riding upon horses, a great company, and a mighty army" (Ezekiel 38:15).

This will not be a normal invasion. The intent of the aggres-sor will be to conquer Israel and destroy it. The bitterness and hatred for the Jewish people, after building up in the Middle East for centuries, will suddenly break loose in a huge onslaught of mounted warriors. From many nations in different parts of the world, including Iran or ancient Persia, and Libya and Ethiopia, they will gather around Gog their leader, "all of them clothed with all sorts of armor, even a great company with bucklers and shields, all of them handling swords" (Ezekiel 38:4–5). And in one gigantic thrust, the invading armies will cover the land like a cloud.

According to Joel's prophecy, it will be a time of great trouble, a day of darkness and gloominess, a day of clouds and of thick-ness darkness. . . . A fire devoureth before them," the prophet says, "and behind them a flame burneth: the land is as the garden of Eden before them, and behind them a desolate wilderness; yea, and nothing shall escape them" (Joel 2:2–3).

But all of this will be to no avail, as far as Gog and his forces are concerned. Eventually, the Lord himself will intervene, and with a rain of hailstones, fire, and brimstone, he will bring the devastating invasion to an end. A countless number of men and animals will fall on that fateful day, and their dead bodies will cover the open fields.

Especially in Jerusalem in the south, there will be a dramatic end to the battle. After being overrun by enemy forces, and at a time when everything appears to be lost, the Jewish people will be delivered in a spectacular and supernatural manner as the Lord Jesus Christ appears and stands upon the Mount of Olives across from the city.

At that moment, according to the book of Zechariah, the mount will cleave in two, one part shifting to the north and the other to the south, providing a miraculous pathway of escape. The captives will flee to the valley of the mountains, and much like the parting of the Red Sea when Moses led the Hebrews out of Egypt, a cataclysmic separation of land will now save a similar group, the embattled inhabitants of Jerusalem and the modern-day descendants of ancient Israel.

This one occurrence, apart from everything else, stands out above all others during the Battle of Armageddon. It is the surprising climax that will bring all fighting and aggression to an end. It is also the event, among many others, that will precede and announce the Second Coming and signal the beginning of the long-awaited Millennium!

Notes

1. Bruce M. Metzger (ed.), Esdras 13:41–45, *The Apocrypha of the Old Testament: Revised Standard Version* (New York: Oxford University Press), p. 65.

2. James E. Talmage, *Conference Report of the Church of Jesus Christ of Latter-day Saints*, April 1916. 13.

3. Joseph Smith, *History of the Church of Jesus Christ of Latter-day Saints*, vol. 1. (Salt Lake City: Deseret Book), 315.

12

EARTHQUAKES AND TRANSFORMATION

The cataclysmic earthquake that will occur at the end of the Battle of Armageddon, splitting the Mount of Olives and freeing the captive people in the city of Jerusalem, will be a tremendous event, causing the earth "to tremble and reel to and fro" and the heavens also to shake (D&C 45:48). Yet it will not match the intensity of two other quakes taking place earlier while the battle is still in process. Both of these quakes occurring in the embattled city and its environs, will cause massive casualties and destruction.

The first will be after Jerusalem has been occupied and under siege for three and a half years, during which time, according to the book of Revelation, two witnesses or prophets will be in the city prophesying about what will soon happen. "These are the two olive trees, and the two candlesticks, standing before the God of the earth" (Revelation 11:4). The men are eventually killed by the people, however, and their dead bodies are purposely left unburied for three and a half days.

Many in the city will rejoice over what has taken place and, as recorded in scripture, will celebrate and send gifts to one another. But after the three and a half days, whatever that time is symbolically meant to be, the two dead prophets suddenly come

71

to life again and stand upon their feet. And in view of all the people, and in response to a voice which is heard from above, they ascend into heaven in a cloud as their enemies below watch them.

It is at this moment that the first of the two huge earthquakes strikes the city, causing much of it to fall in ruins and killing seven thousand people. Those standing nearby are fearful and impressed at what has occurred and give glory to the God of heaven. Yet there is little respite for the people of Jerusalem, for soon after the first quake, the second eventually follows, one allegedly the same as that mentioned in the sixth seal and said to be unprecedented throughout all of human history.

"And there were voices, and thunders, and lightnings," say the scriptures; "and there was a great earthquake, such as was not since men were upon the earth, so mighty an earthquake, and so great. And the great city was divided into three parts, and the cities of the nations fell: and great Babylon came in remembrance before God, to give unto her the cup of the wine of the fierceness of his wrath" (Revelation 16:18–19).

Certainly it will be a historic occasion at that time and a terrifying prelude to when the Lord himself intervenes and brings the Battle of Armageddon to a close. It is also that time in history when earthquakes become continuous and widespread and give notice that the world itself will soon come to an end. Never before have there been such catastrophic conditions.

In connection with these events, the scripture stating that the second quake in Jerusalem will be "such as was not since men were upon the earth" is extremely interesting since it is preceded by so many devastating earthquakes in the past. The deadliest known temblor on record, for example, occurred in the year 1556 in the Shaanxi province in China and reportedly killed 830,000 people. More recently was the giant quake in Chili in 1960, registering 9.5 on the Moment magnitude scale, a type of measurement alleged to be newer and even more accurate than the Richter. This particular earthquake is said to be the largest ever recorded on earth and generated tsunamis all across the Pacific Ocean.[1]

To say there will be another earthquake in years to come, therefore, more powerful than any that have occurred so far gives only a small idea of the incredible shaking that is in store for the earth. But such an event is definitely prophesied, and the gigantic quake described in the book of Revelation will be one without any kind of precedent. Certainly it will be precursor to many others to follow.

Indeed, some of the most prominent prophecies in scripture, and at the same time the most alarming, say that someday there will be a great shaking of the earth, first in the land of Israel and eventually throughout the nations. They predict that not only people and animal life will be affected, but buildings and structures everywhere will be destroyed, along with mountains being thrown down. The countless quakes involved are theoretically the massive aftershocks of the giant earthquakes during the Battle of Armageddon.

"Surely in that day there shall be a great shaking in the land of Israel," according to the Book of Ezekiel, "so that the fishes of the sea, and the fowls of the heaven, and the beasts of the field, and all creeping things that creep upon the earth, and all the men that are upon the face of the earth, shall shake at my presence, and the mountains shall be thrown down, and the steep places shall fall, and every wall shall fall to the ground" (Ezekiel 38:19–20).

In a similar but shorter prophecy in the record of Haggai, the prophet states, "For thus saith the Lord of hosts; Yet once, it is a little while, and I will shake the heavens, and the earth, and the sea, and the dry land; and I will shake all nations" (Haggai 2:6–7).

These prophecies add up to the idea that God himself is not only preparing the nations for the Second Coming but in the process is expressing his displeasure with world conditions and the general attitude of much of the people. Rejection of testimonies given by prophets and emissaries is now resulting in the testimony also given by Deity.

"And after your testimony cometh wrath and indignation upon the people," saith the Lord. "For after your testimony cometh the testimony of earthquakes, that shall cause groanings in the midst of her, and men shall fall upon the ground and shall not be able to stand. And also cometh the testimony of the voice of thunderings, and the voice of lightnings, and the voice of tempests, and the voice of the waves of the sea heaving themselves beyond their bounds. And all things shall be in commotion; and surely men's hearts shall fail them; for fear shall come upon all people.

"And angels shall fly through the midst of heaven, crying with a loud voice, sounding the trump of God, saying: Prepare ye, prepare ye, O inhabitants of the earth; for the judgment of our God is come. Behold, and lo, the Bridegroom cometh; go ye out to meet him" (D&C 88:88–92).

This will come at a time when a ministering of angels is taking place. Following many centuries when no apparent revelation has occurred, the heavens again will be opened with God once more communicating with men on earth. It will be during the lifetimes of men like Joseph Smith who was instrumental in opening a new dispensation of the gospel and restoring the church which existed during the time of Jesus Christ.

Moreover, it will definitely come at a time when natural disasters are increasingly taking place upon the surface of the earth, including the widespread occurrence of earthquakes. Yet all of this is an expression not only of God's wrath and indignation in regard to the people, but in a physical and geological sense also a way of altering and transforming the earth and preparing it for a coming destiny. Predictions and prophecies pertaining to these events are found in scripture, referring first to a shaking and transformation of the earth and then later to a period of burning and cleansing, the former to occur before the Second Coming and the latter to happen after.

The shaking will be in connection with the earth in its temporal and telestial condition and the burning a preparation for one that is temporal and terrestrial or Millennial. Both are necessary in the earth's so-called spiritual progression. The philosophy once again, as explained in scripture, is that the earth itself is a living entity and is necessarily progressing through a series of steps leading to its own salvation and exaltation. As a consequence, the vast burning that occurs in the future will result in new heavens and a new earth, all in preparation for the Millennium.

But a gigantic shaking and rocking of the earth must first take place, and in the scriptures there are many references to what will happen and what the consequences will be. Foremost among these are the prophecies of Isaiah.

"The windows from on high are open," he says, "and the foundations of the earth do shake. The earth is utterly broken down, the earth is clean dissolved, the earth is moved exceedingly. The earth shall reel to and fro like a drunkard, and shall be removed like a cottage" (Isaiah 24:18–20).

In another scripture the prophet gives the well-known description of the consequences. "Every valley shall be exalted," he writes, "and every mountain and hill shall be made low: and the crooked shall be made straight, and the rough places plain: the glory of the Lord shall be revealed, and all flesh shall see it together: for the mouth of the Lord hath spoken it" (Isaiah 40:4–5).

Basically the same thing was recorded by Luke in the New Testament when he said, "Every valley shall be filled, and every mountain and hill shall be brought low; and the crooked shall be made straight, and the rough ways shall be made smooth. And all flesh shall see the salvation of God" (Luke 3:5–6).

In the Doctrine and Covenants, further details are given regarding what will happen in the latter days, especially how the earth will be shaken and appear as one who is drunken and reeling. "Wherefore, be not deceived, but continue in steadfastness," states the scripture, "looking forth for the heavens to be shaken, and the earth to tremble and to reel forth as a drunken man, and for the valleys to be exalted, and for the mountains to be made low, and for the rough places to become smooth—and all this when the angel shall sound his trumpet" (D&C 49:23).

"For not many days hence and the earth shall tremble and reel to and fro as a drunken man," according to still another scripture, "and the sun shall hide his face, and shall refuse to give light; and the moon shall be bathed in blood; and the stars shall become exceedingly angry and shall cast themselves down as a fig that falleth from off a fig tree" (D&C 88:87).

But in Section 133 of the Doctrine and Covenants, an extremely significant statement is made, not only one pertaining to mountains generally being thrown or broken down, but rather a solitary scriptural reference identifying one specific locality involved in a future transformation of the earth.

"And he shall utter voice out of Zion," the scripture says, referring to the Lord, "and he shall speak from Jerusalem, and his voice shall be heard among all people; and it shall be a voice as the voice of many waters, and as the voice of a great thunder, which shall break down the mountains, and the valleys shall not be found. . . . And the land of Jerusalem and the land of Zion shall be turned back into their own place, and the earth shall be like as it was in the day before it was divided" (D&C 133:21–22, 24).

Reference to the lands of Jerusalem and Zion "being turned back into their own place" constitutes a remarkable statement, apparently relating at least in part to the phenomenal shaking and jolting of the earth that is predicted for the future. In order for the earth's geology and surface construction to return to the way it was before it was divided in the days of Peleg, as mentioned in the Bible, tremendous cataclysms without any recorded precedent or parallel must occur.

An example of this type of quaking would be an earthquake similar to the one scheduled to strike Palestine in the waning days of Armageddon, such an earthquake as has never happened before. And yet for the geological and geographical portion of the earth to return to the way it was originally, including the lands of Jerusalem and Zion, a tremendous rocking of the earth will need to take place, not just in one location but many. A theoretical sketch of what the earth's surface looks like beneath the Atlantic and Pacific Oceans, comprising deep chasms and extensive ruptures, gives only a limited idea of what kind of transformation will be necessary to restore the earth to the way it was in the beginning of human history.

When Adam and Eve were in the Garden of Eden, the geography and topography of the earth allegedly were much different from what they are today. In those days, after the waters had been gathered together during the time of the Creation, there was a much smaller volume of seas and ocean. The movement of water, in fact, was generally in one direction and to one specific location, resulting in a much smaller sea. As a consequence, the land surface stretched for thousands of miles in all directions, resulting in what amounted to one gigantic continent.

At that time, the lands of Jerusalem and Zion were still thousands of miles apart, being on opposite sides of the globe, yet no longer separated by water. It would have been possible under those conditions to travel by foot or surface transportation back and forth between the two locations.

Consequently, the assertion that the Garden of Eden was originally where the central part of the United States is now located could very well be true, and had there been the right kinds of transportation anciently, great distances might have been covered in a short period of time. As to whether or not there were mountains to cross, or other such obstacles, that is undetermined.

It is true that Isaiah said that every mountain and hill would be brought low, implying a completely flat land surface, yet the complete meaning of such a statement and description is not known. The important idea is expressed in the Doctrine and Covenants where it says that the earth in the days ahead will be changed and "shall be like as it was in the days before it was divided" (D&C 133:24). What it is that will actually happen on that occasion is not completely known but continues to be an interesting sign of the times. Such events and circumstances have been recorded by the prophets and are timely announced in the annals of scripture!

Notes

1. Wikipedia Encl., http://en.wikipedia.org/wiki/Earthquake.

∞ *13* ∞

SKY AND WATER PHENOMENA

Any sequence in regard to the signs of the times, especially those pertaining to the final part of the last days, is again necessarily tentative and theoretical. Nevertheless, the implication is that sometime toward the end of this period, there will occur in the sky miraculous phenomena involving the sun, moon, and stars. This is a concept stating that the first two of these entities will be darkened someday, and the third will fall from the sky.

It is also a subject often spoken of in scripture but seldom understood. Indeed, in very few places is there a sign of the times that is more enigmatic and puzzling than this one. It is a concept vacillating between the factual and realistic, and the figurative or symbolic. But it is an important sign nonetheless and, in one way or another, will definitely happen.

The idea is introduced in the twenty-fourth chapter of Matthew when Jesus answered a question asked by his disciples. "What shall be the sign of thy coming," they said, "and of the end of the world?" Jesus then informed them that certain events needed to occur before his second advent, including wars and rumors of wars, earthquakes in different places, famines, and pestilence. He also said that the gospel would first be preached throughout the world. It was then that he told them about the sun, moon, and stars, and the sign of the Son of man.

"Immediately after the tribulation of those days shall the sun be darkened," he said, "and the moon shall not give her light, and the stars shall fall from heaven, and the powers of the heavens shall be shaken: and then shall appear the sign of the Son of man in heaven: and then shall all the tribes of the earth mourn, and they shall see the Son of man coming in the clouds of heaven with power and great glory" (Matthew 24:29–30).

In this preliminary report, the most surprising thing was undoubtedly the idea that stars would fall from heaven, certainly a remarkable statement. It was also mentioned that the sun would be darkened and the moon would refuse to give light, all of which are miraculous occurrences.

Many times in regard to scripture, however, it is a matter of deciding whether or not the wording denotes a literal occurrence or one that is figurative or symbolic. And in the instances of stars falling out of the sky and the moon refusing to give light, or on occasion turning to blood, obviously a symbolic meaning is generally intended. Stars being planets, in other words, do not normally plummet through space like meteors, nor will the moon change into a different substance. Nevertheless, a particular prophet who sometimes makes such statements, and even the Lord on occasion, is effective in using this type of language, and his point is usually well taken.

Whatever the scriptural wording might be, the concept pertaining to the darkening or coloring of the sun and moon is interesting, and the type of language involved is usually understandable and acceptable. It is the statements referring to the stars that are particularly significant, not only concerning the stars themselves, but the constellations as well. In the Book of Isaiah, for example, the prophet says that in the last days "the stars of heaven and the constellations thereof shall not give their light: the sun shall be darkened in his going forth, and the moon shall not cause her light to shine" (Isaiah 13:10).

The fact that Isaiah is the only prophet who refers to the constellations is noteworthy. And although he says nothing about them being in motion, only that they will refuse to give light, the idea is still important, suggesting that both they and the sun, moon, and individual stars will be perceived as performing in unexpected ways, consequently resulting in visual effects that will be significant signs of the times.

A person needs only to look at a map of the constellations in the two hemispheres to visualize what it would be like on future occasions if it appears that the constellations are moving or are in commotion. If only twelve of them, for example, such as those associated with the signs of the Zodiac, were observed at nighttime to be in some kind of disorder or confusion, along with their individual stars, it would naturally be a sign that something extremely important was about to take place, something that had never happened before. And indeed just such a thing has been prophesied to occur in the future, namely that the stars in the heavens will be in disarray, showing that a countdown of critical events has begun and that the Second Coming is on its way!

In addition to the prophecy of Isaiah, there are other scriptures relating to the stars and the unusual language used in their description. It is some of the figurative expressions that are particularly interesting. The portrayal of stars becoming "exceedingly angry" and casting themselves down as recorded in the Doctrine and Covenants, for example, illustrates the use of literary personification, as does their refusal to shine. Instances saying that stars "fell unto the earth" (Revelation 6:13) or were "hurled from their places" (D&C 133:49) also show an abnormal use of language as far as heavenly bodies is concerned. The different kinds of literary devices used by the prophets and authors of scripture are many.

"For not many days hence and the earth shall tremble and reel to and fro as a drunken man," the record says, as shown in the Doctrine and Covenants, "and the sun shall hide his face, and shall refuse to give light; and the moon shall be bathed in blood; and the stars shall become exceedingly angry, and shall cast themselves down as a fig that falleth off a fig-tree" (D&C 88:87). In the book of Revelation there is similar wording which states that "the stars of heaven fell unto the earth, even as a fig tree casteth her untimely figs, when she is shaken of a mighty wind" (Revelation 6:13).

Moreover, there are those scriptures which suggest that the phenomena of sun, moon, and stars will not only be a preliminary sign of the Lord's Second Coming but also one relating to his Millennial reign on earth. "Then the moon shall be confounded," says Isaiah, "and the sun ashamed, when the Lord of hosts shall reign in mount Zion, and in Jerusalem, and before his ancients gloriously" (Isaiah 24:23). Also in modern scripture in reference to the Lord, it says that "so great shall be the glory of his presence that the sun shall hide his face in shame, and the moon shall withhold its light, and the stars shall be hurled from their places" (D&C 133:49).

Again the variety of references to the sun, moon, and stars constitutes a significant body of material, and it has prompted considerable comment and opinion among many who read and study the scriptures. Some regard the prophecies as events yet to come, whereas others are inclined to say they have already been partially fulfilled. Because of pollutants in the air, for example, along with other factors pertaining to a modern technology, there have been times when the sun has been abnormally darkened, and certain chemicals in the air have sometimes given the moon an unusual reddish color. During violent earthquakes, which have been many, it might have seemed on occasion during nighttime that stars were falling or were in motion.

But impressive as these phenomena might be, they still are not the signs of the times mentioned in the scriptures. On the occasions of their occurrence, they have had a significant impact on those who have seen them, but these events have undoubtedly never reached the level of magnificence which would equate them with what the Bible and other scriptures are talking about. Also such things as a large volume of recorded UFO occurrences, regarded at times not only as abnormalities in the sky but as signs or omens, do not qualify.

It might rightfully be said, therefore, that when the sun is darkened in a scriptural sense becoming "black as sackcloth of hair," when the moon is reddened enough to be associated with blood, and when an unusually large number of meteorites fall to the earth causing an untold amount of damage, only then can it be said that a most extraordinary event has happened for the first time and a religious prophecy has been fulfilled. In other words, something much more than what modern technology can create, as sophisticated as it has become, will be needed to bring about a realization and fulfillment of the remarkable statements recorded in scripture.

The same might be said in connection with what is referred to as the sign of the Son of man, especially in regard to this particular occurrence. The only place where this scripture is recorded in the Bible is in the twenty-fourth chapter of Matthew in the New Testament, yet it is possibly enough to position it chronologically and differentiate it from other occurrences.

"Immediately after the tribulation of those days shall the sun be darkened," the scripture says, "and the moon shall not give her light, and the stars shall fall from heaven, and the powers of the heavens shall be shaken. And then shall appear the sign of the Son of man in heaven: and then shall the tribes of the earth mourn, and they shall see the Son of man coming in the clouds of heaven with power and great glory" (Matthew 24:29–30). There is also a very brief scripture in the Doctrine and Covenants which states that all people shall see the sign together (D&C 88:93), all of which poses the question as to what type of sign it will be and how it will differ from other phenomena in the sky.

Any answer to such a question is elusive. The only clue is that it will follow soon after what happens to the sun, moon, and stars and will possibly be very close in time to the Second Coming itself. Some might claim to have seen it after witnessing an impressive display of comets or meteors, or other such phenomena, yet the implication of the prophecy is that this is an event that will be extraordinary and without any precedent or parallel.

In reality, it could turn out to be a quiet, subtle event, more impressive because of its meaning and significance rather than any striking astronomic or stellar occurrence. But whatever it might be, and whenever it occurs, it will be one of the final signs of the times, a part of the final countdown of events that will eventually lead to the opening of heaven and the Second Coming of Jesus Christ!

Undoubtedly it will be a strategic and dramatic time in history, and as the time draws closer to a conclusion of the countdown, the essence of the moment becomes especially urgent and significant. There is an increased awareness that something unprecedented and momentous is about to happen. Everything implies some kind of ending or conclusion. And yet before any final event takes place as forecast in scripture, a phenomenon relating to water must first occur, particularly as it pertains to the seas and oceans. The transformation of the earth must finally be accomplished and the water and land surfaces returned to the way they were in the beginning. A level of completeness and fulfillment needs to be attained. And the most reliable source of information for this important historical period, both as to time and sequence, is again the record of scripture known as the Doctrine and Covenants.

"And he shall utter his voice out of Zion, and he shall speak from Jerusalem," the records states, referring to the Lord, "and his voice shall be heard among all people; and it shall be a voice as the voice of many waters, and as the voice of a great thunder, which shall break down the mountains, and the valleys shall not be found. He shall command the great deep, and it shall be driven back into the north countries, and the islands shall become one land; and the land of Jerusalem and the land of Zion shall be turned back into their own place, and the earth shall be like as it was in the days before it was divided" (D&C 133:23–24).

This particular scripture, noted for its brevity in covering so many important events, describes the occurrences and circumstances taking place a short time before the Millennium, namely those leading up to the inevitable climax known as the end of the world. The sequence of what will happen is not entirely clear, yet there is an implication that a definite sequence does exist. In connection with the massive string of earthquakes, for example, that are scheduled to shake the earth, it is logical that a transformation and restructuring will take place during that period of time. This is when mountains will fall all across the planet, and the topography of the earth's surface will become increasingly more level and much like a plain.

Then at a later time, theoretically following the phenomena in the sky relating to the sun, moon, and stars, the waters of the great deep will be driven back into the north country, and the earth's land surface will be transformed into a single continent adjoining a much smaller area of water. And although the scripture in the Doctrine and Covenants at first might suggest that a transformation of land occurs after the water action, logic again would say it will happen before, at the time of the earthquakes! First comes the geologic change, and then the hydraulic.

In any case, this event brings the world toward the end of the final countdown. At a time in history when a tremendous shaking of the planet has resulted in a restructuring and transformation of the earth's land surface, and after the phenomena relating to the sky has taken place, as well as the sign of the Son of man, it is that time also when a huge volume of sea and ocean will recede into the north countries to be driven, as it were, to a new location. On that occasion, the areas of Jerusalem and Palestine in the east and the city and land of Zion in the west will "be turned back into their own place," the result of a giant recession of water as well as geologic transformation, and the earth will become like it was in the days before it was divided.

Certainly these will be remarkable and miraculous events, including the one pertaining to water. To visualize a large part of the Pacific and Atlantic Oceans, along with their adjacent seas, all referred to scripturally as the "waters of the great deep," relocating someday to the north and at the same time resulting in a much lower sea level is very difficult to understand without knowing some kind of meaningful reason or purpose. Merely to say that a huge volume of water will turn northward without any place to go when it gets there does not hold with reality. Consequently, there has to be some kind of explanation, and as it turns out, it is found not only in the statement in the Doctrine and Covenants that talks about the earth and the time before it was divided but is implied also in a reference to the division of the earth mentioned in the book of Genesis in the Bible.

In the tenth chapter of Genesis, in the twenty-fifth verse, an unusual and controversial scripture is recorded. "And unto Eber were born two sons: the name of the one was Peleg; for in his days was the earth divided; and his brother's name was Joktan."

That is all that is said about it. There is no further information given. It is though a sudden thought were suddenly sandwiched between two relatively unimportant items of genealogy for some unknown purpose. Consequently, the scripture has generated considerable conjecture and speculation as to what is actually meant by a division of the earth.

What kind of division was the ancient prophet and historian of Genesis talking about when he said the earth was divided? What purpose did it serve to introduce this kind of topic so dramatically and unexpectedly? Regarding these questions, many answers have been given, with historians and biblical scholars differing so widely that any consensus of opinion appears unlikely.

Yet there is possibly a correct answer, one which explains the mysterious recession of seas and oceans into the north country, at the same time giving important scriptural evidence and information that provide an interesting adjunct to the signs of the times.

In the Bible, for example, several meanings have been given to the statement that the earth was divided in the days of Peleg. All of these relate in one way or another to the etymology of Peleg's name, which in the Hebrew language signifies watercourse and division. Whatever it was that happened in his day, it was an important event, enough so that he was named after it.

A statement in the first book of Chronicles, almost identical to the one in Genesis except for the word "because," states very clearly the reason for such a name. "And unto Eber were born two sons: the name of the one was Peleg; because in his days the earth was divided: and his brother's name was Joktan" (1 Chronicles 1:19).

The important question once again is what is meant by the word "divided?" What happened in ancient times that prompted such an unusual term or expression? Moreover, was the event something that should be considered literally, or just figuratively and symbolically, and how might it relate to a tremendous volume of water being driven to the northern part of the globe? Such a brief reference in scripture obviously creates a problem, as well as a question, and consequently there is a good number of theories or explanations, one of which might present a solution.

(1) The most prominent theory, and the one most prevalent in the literature, is that divided refers to a division of people. A few verses following the passage of scripture in Genesis relating to Peleg, for example, the text reads as follows: "These are the families of the sons of Noah, after their generations, in their nations: and by these were the nations divided in the earth after the flood" (Genesis

10:32). Certainly the wording suggests some type of division.

(2) Another interpretation is that word "divided" refers to the time when Peleg and Joktan separated and went in different directions, the first apparently remaining in Mesopotamia and the latter migrating southward into the Arabian Peninsula.

(3) A third explanation pertains to a political and geographical division of territory. It might have involved the establishment of certain types of territorial limits or municipal boundaries at the time, but whatever it was, if it actually happened when Peleg was born, it evidently had an important impact on a large population of people.

(4) There is also the idea that the division of the earth referred to irrigation and agriculture. The etymology of Peleg's name, having to do with water as well as division, and consequently related to such terms as "watercourse, canal, and channel," might have been associated with people in Mesopotamia beginning the construction of extensive irrigation canals.

(5) Another meaning of "divided" is that it was the conclusion of the great Flood during the time of Noah. Instead of water rapidly draining off from the earth, as recorded in the Bible, it is suggested that it receded much more slowly, eventually stopping during the days of Peleg, at which time the division of land into islands and continents finally became complete.

Along with these interpretations, several minor ones exist, yet there are still two other important possibilities remaining, each of which constitutes an interesting theory and explanation. The first of these affirms that in the days of Peleg, the earth as one huge landmass was divided into different segments that started drifting apart, eventually forming the continents and islands as they exist today. And whereas the theory of drifting continents is today generally accepted by the scientific community and is referred to as plate tectonics, it does not apply to the time of Peleg, having taken place many millions of years ago.

And finally there is a second interpretation, one found in modern scripture and existing in a very unexpected place, hidden away, as it were, in a remote and secluded location. Very brief in content, it occurs suddenly and unexpectedly, much like its companion material in the Bible.

There are only two verses of biblical scripture, one in Genesis and the other in First Chronicles, that mention the division of the earth during the days of Peleg. Extremely brief and ambiguous, they have long been a puzzle to biblical scholars and have often resulted in significant problems. Ironically, there is the same number of verses in the Doctrine and Covenants, just as brief in wording and content, that refer to this same event. And it is this last piece of information that finally unravels the mystery of what the account in the Bible pertaining to a division of the earth actually means. Besides explaining the word "divided" itself, relating it specifically to a large deluge of water, these two verses of scripture also establish the cause of the deluge, as well as its geographical source!

Referring to the latter days and a time preceding the Second Coming, the verses read as follows: "He shall command the great deep, and it shall be driven back into the north countries, and the islands shall become one land. And the land of Jerusalem and the land of Zion shall be turned back into their own place, and the earth shall be like as it was in the days before it was divided" (D&C 133:23–24).

This one scripture, providing valuable information and insight, answers several puzzling questions. First, the division of the earth in Peleg's time was the result of incoming water, an extreme flooding of the land, much like the flood during the days of Noah although much less extensive, which created the outline and perimeter of hundreds of islands and seven continents.

Second, the statement that water "shall be driven back into the north countries" is a strong implication that that is where it came from in the first place, originating somewhere in the northern part of the globe, apparently in places of outlet permitting the effluence of huge amounts of subterranean water. It came down from the north, in other words, and it will someday go back to the north. Within the context of this scripture, water "gathered together unto one place," as described in the biblical account of Creation, takes on a different significance, or at least a double meaning and second interpretation.

Third, it is especially important, after the many opinions that have been given, to learn more about the word "divided" as it is used in the books of Genesis and First Chronicles. There appears to be considerable evidence now that the term in question refers to a remarkable deluge during the days of Peleg, reminiscent also of the time of the Creation and the great Flood in the days of Noah!

Finally, there is again the question of where water will go after it is driven into the north countries, a question at present having no definite answer. All that can be said is that it remains one of the mysteries of this particular area of the globe. Yet there are theories and speculation that somewhere in the far north, the earth has the hydraulic capacity to emit and absorb huge quantities of subterranean water. With what happened at the time of Creation and in the days of Noah serving as precedents, the phenomenon of water emerging onto the earth during the time of Peleg definitely approaches reality, a situation in which the water involved will someday be driven back again to the north where it first appeared

This means that three times during the world's human history, water has emerged from subterranean reservoirs and covered all or part of the earth's surface. Twice it has receded and returned to its original location. And once again, during a time in the latter days shortly before the Second Coming of Jesus Christ, it will recede one last time as the waters of the great deep respond to a divine command and are driven back into the north countries.

The wording in the Doctrine and Covenants saying that water will be driven back is obviously different and unconventional. The meaning of the language solicits a variety of opinions. One idea, for example, referring to water moving to the north, is that there will be a thunderous noise as an entire ocean relocates, associating the account with an adjoining scripture that refers to "the voice of many waters."

This kind of action, however, is undoubtedly too dramatic, a more plausible occurrence being that the receding water will follow more closely what took place when waters were gathered together during the Creation and after the great Flood. On those occasions, at least in Noah's time, it took five or five and a half months for floodwaters to recede, and a similar amount of time might be involved when water originating during the time of Peleg returns to the north country.

This means that in the future, after the surface of the earth has been restructured and transformed by way of earthquakes, further changes will occur via the eroding and sculpting effects of water as it returns to its original source, everything being prepared for an eventual burning and cleansing at the end of the world. Simultaneously, people will continue the process of everyday living, observing the many changes taking place during an undetermined period of time. Following the Battle of Armageddon, for example, it will take seven months to bury the dead, according to the Bible, and seven years to burn the weapons of war and refuse, many other events undoubtedly taking place during this time period. Concluding events and circumstances will most likely be varied and unusual while others will probably continue as in the past. Prior to the time of the Second Coming, people will be doing what they have always done, and then one day, suddenly and unexpectedly, the end will come!

In the meantime, the division of the earth in the days of Peleg is an important milestone of the past, one in which new waterways among seven continents and countless islands became highways, as it were, for future migration and colonization. In those days, the world was on the verge of a new era of discovery and at the threshold of fortune and destiny which lay ahead. It was a new world of adventure and opportunity. And inevitably on the distant horizon, as men and ships crossed new seas and oceans, there were also those future events, pending and waiting, that ultimately would lead to the end of human affairs on a telestial earth and provide a gateway to the Millennium!

14

THE CURTAIN OF
HEAVEN

Among the concluding events of a final countdown, and
after the many occurrences that have taken place, the precise moment arrives when the curtain of heaven is finally to be
unfolded. The most important event in human history, other than
the Atonement and Resurrection, is now scheduled to occur. At
some location in relation to the earth, in an area undetermined,
Jehovah in the person of Jesus Christ will suddenly make an
appearance that has been announced and previewed for six millennia, an event prophesied by countless prophets in the past and
one anticipated by righteous people in all ages and eras of time.
Indeed, it is at this exact period in time that the Second Coming
will take place, and a new beginning and lifetime will commence.

At the conclusion of six remarkable events of countdown, some
of them almost unbelievable in their conditions and circumstances,
the last step is ready to begin. The crowning event and climax
before Christ's second advent and the most important momentous
occurrence since the meridian of time is about to commence. All
that has happened so far is merely a prelude to what now takes
place.

According to a prescribed time, which Jesus on one occasion
said was known only to his Father, the curtain of heaven is suddenly

unfolded and raised. In a manner unidentified and unexplained, the covering obstructing a view of heaven is removed, and the Lord's presence will be revealed. Certainly it is difficult to describe what actually happens at this time, and scriptures relating to it at first seem ambiguous and confusing. Indeed a description of this particular event in the book of Revelation has been referred to as a very difficult expression. It is especially difficult when associated with a scroll. "And the heaven departed," the scripture says, "as a scroll when it is rolled together" (Revelation 6:14).

An initial reading of this verse presents a picture of heaven leaving, much like a written scroll disappearing from view when it is rolled up. Again it is a difficult image to visualize and a hard one to understand, and because of this there are undoubtedly many opinions.

The correct image, however, is one that is in direct opposition to a scroll being rolled up, rather one where it is opened or undone, after it has been rolled together. Instead of the sky being viewed symbolically as a pliant or flexible expanse which can be rolled together, the meaning in the scripture is that the heavens will be opened. Joseph Smith was of this opinion also when he interpreted Revelation 6:14, saying, "And the heavens opened as a scroll is opened when it is rolled together" (JST Revelation 6:14).

The meaning of this type of wording is further complicated by a similar usage in the book of Isaiah where the prophet writes, "And all the host of heaven shall be dissolved, and the heavens shall be rolled together as a scroll" (Isaiah 34:4). And although the wording is similar, it apparently has a very different interpretation, one relating to the dissolution of the heavens and the creation of new heavens and a new earth.

Finally, it is in another record, the Doctrine and Covenants, where clear and unmistakable language depicts what will actually occur in regard to the curtain of heaven. In brief but certain terms, the vocabulary and phrasing in the book of Revelation are paraphrased and explained.

"And there shall be silence in heaven for the space of half an hour, the record says; "and immediately after shall the curtain of heaven be unfolded, as a scroll is unfolded after it is rolled up, and the face of the Lord shall be unveiled" (D&C 88:95).

The point in all of this, of course, is that this again is the time in history when the Second Coming of Jesus Christ occurs, the calendar date also for the approach of the biblical Millennium. This is not the time of the giant holocaust and burning which later takes place on the earth's surface, but rather the resplendent time of resurrection that precedes it. It is only after the latter has happened that the worldwide burning of the planet will occur.

Surely this will be a time of celebration for those who have led righteous lives, yet at the same time one of mourning and remorse for those who have done otherwise. It is that time in world history when the clock stops, as it were, and the Lord makes his first official appearance among the people, a time when all of the righteous, both the living and the dead, are called up to meet him in the clouds of glory. Then according to the right time and sequence, at a time designated as the end of the world, the earth finally will be burned and cleansed. It is at this time that a second genesis occurs and also a brand new beginning, one with an entirely new social order, as well as one that is political, and mankind for the first time will know what it is like to be in the Millennium!

15

THE MORNING OF THE FIRST RESURRECTION

Deity has made it clear, and has given it as a caveat or warning, that the Second Coming will occur unexpectedly, and by analogy will come as a thief during the nighttime when most people are supposedly asleep. The implication is that it will definitely occur when they least expect it. Indeed the cautioning forecast has been given many times, and the admonition has always been for people to be prepared and ready, and continually aware of the signs of the times.

"Even so it shall be in that day when they shall see all these things," referring to the many signs," then shall they know that the hour is nigh. And it shall come too pass that he that feareth me shall be looking forth for the great day of the Lord to come, even for the signs of the coming of the Son of Man" (D&C 45:38–39). "And again, verily I say unto you, the coming of the Lord draweth nigh, and it overtaketh the world as a thief in the night" (D&C 106:4).

At a certain moment in the future, therefore, the opening of the curtain of heaven will finally occur. The indication is that there will be an initial signal, apparently the sound of a trumpet sounding long and loud, announcing that something of great importance is about to take place. The sounding of trumpets has been used many times in initiating important occurrences and preparing the way for what is to come, and now at this time, it is again the preparatory signal. At this particular moment, it is allegedly the first sound people will hear, causing all throughout the nations to stop suddenly and look toward the sky.

Certainly it will be a sound like no other, and although it will be audible to everyone in the world and cause them to tremble, it is uncertain how many will witness visually what now takes place. But the promise has been given, and it is one recorded in scripture, that the Lord will descend from above, coming "in the clouds of heaven, clothed with power and great glory" (D&C 45:44). Accompanying him will be many others, including a large host of heavenly angels.

Instantaneously, the righteous people living on earth who qualify for entrance into that part of heaven known as the Celestial Kingdom are quickened and caught up to meet them. At the same time, the graves in countless places around the world will suddenly be opened, and an incredible number of people, most of whom have been dead for centuries and qualify for the Celestial Kingdom, will be resurrected and caught up to join the heavenly throng!

In no time or place is there anything that can compare with what happens on this occasion. No written or spoken description will ever be adequate in attempting to tell what now takes place. To visualize the human drama occurring all across the globe as literally millions or billions of people are caught up to meet Jehovah, or Jesus Christ, is understandably beyond any comprehension. Everything taking place will be entirely without any kind of parallel or precedent.

But it will all happen, and in the process a sociality down through the ages will be resumed among the people of the earth. For the first time in an earthly setting, after an absence of many decades and centuries, people will resume where they left off, as it were, at the same time looking forward to the future. Yet at a specific moment, as they come into the presence of him who has made this glorious transformation and reunion possible, they will join with others in expressing worship and gratitude.

It is an unprecedented moment, and logically everything happening will be transacted not only individually but mainly by families, both by those who are living and those resurrected from the dead. In few places in scripture or otherwise is there anything conclusive as to what will actually occur, but the idea that things will be conducted at a family level is appropriate and reasonable. At the time that righteous people who are alive are quickened and caught up to meet Jehovah, infants and children of all ages will be accompanied by their parents, or by other adults in the family organization. The same will be true with children and adults in the resurrection, everything taking place under the auspices of the family.

One of the revelations that Joseph Smith received, as recorded in the Doctrine and Covenants, states that all children who die before the age of accountability, which is eight years of age, need no baptism and automatically become eligible to enter the Celestial Kingdom, meaning the Kingdom of Heaven (D&C 137:10). This means that on the Morning of the First Resurrection, as Jesus descends from above, an untold number of children under eight years of age will be resurrected and caught up to meet him. Some of these theoretically will not be accompanied by parents, but by other family members, and the thoughts of so many children, including infants that must be carried, coming forth at this time again might be very difficult to visualize.

Possibly no other event during the Second Coming will be as dramatic and impressive as this one. Indeed, young people coming forth at this time are individuals who as adults in premortality had been righteous and worthy but for whatever reason were not given the opportunity to live more than a brief time on earth. Yet whatever their particular circumstances might be, they are not to be penalized. Because of their individual circumstances and worthiness, they will now be heirs to the Kingdom of Heaven, and in the days ahead during the time of the Millennium, they will grow and develop to a certain age of adulthood and live forever in the presence of God (D&C 63:51).

Concerning this time, it is interesting to note something Joseph Smith told a woman who had lost a young child in death. Both she and another woman were grieving over children that had died early, and the Prophet gave them these words of comfort. "He told us that we should receive those children in the morning of the resurrection," the first one said, "just as we laid them down, in purity and innocence, and we should nourish and care for them as their mothers. He said that children would be raised in the resurrection just as they were laid down, and that they would obtain all the intelligence necessary to occupy thrones, principalities, and powers."[1]

On another occasion, the Prophet in conversing with someone else who had lost an infant child told her "she should have the joy, the pleasure, and the satisfaction of rearing that child, after the resurrection, until it reached the full stature of its spirit; and that it would be a far greater joy than she could possibly have in mortality, because she would be free from the sorrow and fear and disabilities of mortal life, and she would know more than she could know in this life."[2]

Surely it must be reassuring for people to know that life will not only continue beyond the grave, but the type of experience and sociality that exists here will also exist there at a much higher level. This will include the opportunity of raising children who never had the experience of childhood and adulthood on earth but will have it in the resurrection, at the same time strengthening the family relationship. For most people, to know this and anticipate it will be a matter of greatest importance.

Moreover, it is also important to know about the resurrection itself, including the curtain of heaven and its raising or opening, or whatever it is that will permit the face of the Lord to be unveiled and revealed. It is especially important to know what the scriptures say concerning this momentous occurrence.

Very little is said in the Bible about the Lord appearing in the clouds of heaven, and technically nothing about the idea of a curtain. The gospel of Matthew in the New Testament is one of the few referring to this outstanding event. "And then shall appear the sign of the Son of man in heaven," the scripture says, "and then shall all the tribes of the earth mourn, and they shall see the Son of man coming in the clouds of heaven with power and great glory. And he shall send his angels with a great sound of a trumpet, and they shall gather together his elect from the four winds, from one end of heaven to the other" (Matthew 24:30–31).

As to the details of what will happen at this time, referring specifically to the resurrection, it is only in modern scripture that various accounts are given. In the Doctrine Covenants, for example, both the curtain and the resurrection are mentioned. "And there shall be silence in heaven for half an hour; and immediately after shall the curtain of heaven be unfolded, as a scroll is unfolded after it is rolled up, and the face of the Lord shall be unveiled.

"And the saints that are upon the earth, who are alive, shall be quickened and be caught up to meet him. And they who have slept in their graves shall come forth, for their graves shall be opened; and they also shall be caught up to meet him in the midst of the pillar of heaven. They are Christ's, the first fruits, they who shall descend with him first, and they who are on the earth and in their graves, who are first caught up to meet him; and all this by the voice of the sounding of the trump of the angel of God" (D&C 88:95–98).

In a further account, the resurrection of righteous people who are heirs to the Kingdom of Heaven is described, an event to occur before any burning of the earth takes place. " And then they shall look for me," the Lord says, "and behold I will come; and they shall see me in the clouds of heaven, clothed with power and great glory; with all the holy angels; and he that watches not for me shall be cut off. But before the arm of the Lord shall fall," referring to a worldwide burning and holocaust, "an angel shall sound his trump, and the saints that have slept shall come forth to meet me in the cloud.

"Wherefore, if ye have slept in peace blessed are you; for as ye now behold me and know that I am, even so shall ye come unto me and your souls shall live, and your redemption shall be perfected; and the saints shall come forth from the four quarters of the earth. Then shall the arm of the Lord fall upon the nations" (D&C 45:44–47).

In still another scripture, one that refers to a veil or covering, mention is again made to what amounts to a curtain. "Behold, it is my will," saith the Lord, "that all they who call on my name, and worship me according to mine everlasting gospel, should gather together, and stand in holy places; and prepare for the revelation which is to come, when the veil of the covering of my temple, in my tabernacle, which hideth the earth, shall be taken off, and all flesh shall see me together" (D&C 101:22–23).

At the time of the Second Coming, therefore, the veil of the temple in heaven, which separates the most holy place from the world without, will be taken off. And although the wording in the scripture is not entirely clear, the "veil of the covering" apparently is synonymous with the "curtain of heaven" in another scripture, where the curtain is unfolded, as a scroll is unfolded after it is rolled up. In any case, the important meaning involved is that following the passage of many centuries, the obstruction between earth and heaven will finally be removed and the face of the Lord will be unveiled.

In a concluding scripture, an account is given which includes the early apostles who were with Jesus during the time of his earthly ministry, people who will also be with him at the time of his coming. "For the hour is nigh," he said, "and that which was spoken by mine apostles must be fulfilled; for as they spoke so shall it come to pass; for I will reveal myself from heaven with power and great glory, with all the hosts thereof, and dwell in righteousness with men on earth a thousand years, and the wicked shall not stand.

"And again, verily, verily, I say unto you, and it hath gone forth in a firm decree, by the will of the Father, that mine apostles, the Twelve which were with me in my ministry at Jerusalem, shall stand at my right hand at the day of my coming in a pillar of fire, being clothed with robes of righteousness, with crowns upon their heads, in glory even as I am, to judge the whole house of Israel, even as many as have loved me and kept my commandments, and none else.

"For a trump shall sound both long and loud, even as upon Mount Sinai, and all the earth shall quake, and they shall come forth—yea, even the dead which died in me, to receive a crown of righteousness, and to be clothed upon, even as I am, to be with me, that we may be one" (D&C 29:10–13).

Again all of this will occur at the same time that righteous people living on earth are also caught up to meet the Lord and the incoming heavenly throng, which one scripture says will comprise "ten thousands of his saints" (Jude 14). Certainly it will be a remarkable occasion, and the fact that the original apostles will be with Jesus, standing at his right hand, gives added emphasis to what is taking place. The reference to them arriving together in a pillar of fire is particularly impressive.

Too much cannot be said in praise and wonder concerning these miraculous events. The morning of the first resurrection will be replete with occurrences of unparalleled significance. The spectacle of millions of children coming forth at this time, for example, an untold number of whom will undoubtedly have to be carried, presents an almost overwhelming scene. At the time that Jesus was resurrected in Jerusalem, many of the saints arose from the dead and went into the holy city, appearing unto many, but for an untold number of children, along with all of those who accompany them, to come forth on this later occasion is again almost beyond any imagination and comprehension. Surely in and of itself, it will be an ultimate climax!

Notes

1. Joseph Smith, *History of the Church of Jesus Christ of Latter-day Saints*, vol. 4. (Salt Lake City: Deseret Book), 556.

2. Joseph F. Smith, "Status of Children in the Resurrection," *Improvement Era*, May 1918. 571.

16

THE CELESTIAL KINGDOM

In the restoration of the church in the latter days, accomplished through the instrumentality of Joseph Smith, the Prophet received another unusual revelation pertaining to those who would be heirs to the Kingdom of Heaven. It stated that in addition to children who died before reaching eight years of age, in the past as well as in the future, all worthy people that died without a knowledge of the gospel, who would have received it had they been given an opportunity, would also be heirs to that kingdom. It was an extraordinary declaration and revelation to the world and undoubtedly gave hope and assurance to a tremendous number of people.

The revelation at first might appear to be in opposition to the scripture in the Bible which says that unless a person is born of the water and of the Spirit, he or she cannot enter the kingdom of God. This was a principle introduced by Jesus when he talked with Nicodemus at one time, affirming that unless one is baptized in the correct manner and according to the correct authority, there will be no entrance into that kingdom. Consequently, this raises the question as to whether or not those who are heirs, and are beyond eight years old, need to be baptized .

In connection with this ordinance, therefore, an important doctrine of the latter-day church is that if a worthy person dies without baptism, someone on earth can go to a temple and be baptized for him or her by proxy, thus satisfying the requirement stated to Nicodemus. In this way, people who die without a knowledge of the gospel and are heirs to the kingdom of God because of worthiness can receive the benefit of baptism. Certainly, it is an important and significant principle pertaining to personal salvation and the process of resurrection.

Also, it is interesting that there is only one place in the Bible that mentions baptism for the dead, albeit it is an extremely important principle. It is found in the first epistle the Apostle Paul wrote to the Corinthians. Referring to the resurrection, he said, "Else what shall they do who are baptized for the dead, if the dead rise not at all? Why are they then baptized for the dead?" (1 Corinthians 15:29).

As with the biblical scriptures relating to Peleg and the division of the earth, along with the companion scripture in the Doctrine and Covenants, the one pertaining to baptism for the dead is likewise extremely noteworthy. Definitely there is the implication that this unusual ordinance was practiced in Paul's day and very likely during other time periods as well. It is another example of something of great importance isolated and set apart in scripture for whatever reason, the complete significance of which to be divulged or revealed at a later time.

All of this suggests that in the morning of the first resurrection, people coming forth from their graves will have been baptized personally or by someone who has been baptized for them, or will be at a suitable time, all in accordance with what has been outlined in scripture. It will be a situation where not only logic and reason will prevail, but also the benevolence of God.

It also presents an interesting question of what life will be like in the hereafter, particularly in the highest realm of heaven, or the Celestial Kingdom. Where is this area located, for example, and what are some of the existing conditions and circumstances?

There is also a question in relation to the word "celestial" itself, a term rarely occurring in the Bible.

In the first epistle to the Corinthians, located only a few verses from the reference to baptism for the dead, there is the following scripture. "All flesh is not the same flesh," the record says; "but there is one kind of flesh of men, another flesh of beasts, another of fishes, and another of birds. There are also celestial bodies, and bodies terrestrial: but the glory of the celestial is one, and the glory of the terrestrial is another.

"There is one glory of the sun, and another glory of the moon, and another glory of the stars: for one star differs from another star in glory. So also is the resurrection of the dead" (1 Corinthians 15:39–42).

The biblical terminology of "celestial" appearing for the first time is highly unusual. It is as though it had been omitted from the Bible elsewhere for some unknown reason, the same applying to the word "terrestrial." Yet both obviously pertain to areas and conditions of utmost importance, signifying places of distinction and glory. In addition, along with a third area of glory, the groups are compared with the sun, moon, and stars respectively.

Again it is only in modern scripture where a further explanation of this is recorded. In the 76th Section of the Doctrine and Covenants, for example, a detailed definition is given for the three kingdoms in heaven known as the Celestial, Terrestrial, and Telestial. Each is referred to as a kingdom of glory, yet it is only the Celestial Kingdom where God resides that will be the residence for those who are heirs to the Kingdom of Heaven, a partial description of which is as follows.

"These shall dwell in the presence of God and his Christ forever and ever. These are they whom he shall bring with him, when he shall come in the clouds of heaven to reign on the earth over his people.

"These are they who shall have part in the first resurrection. These are they who shall come forth in the resurrection of the just. These are they who are come unto Mount Zion, and unto the city of the living God, the heavenly place, the holiest of all.

"These are they who have come to an innumerable company of angels, to the general assembly and church of Enoch, and of the Firstborn. These are they whose names are written in heaven, where God and Christ are the judge of all."

"These are they whose bodies are celestial, whose glory is that of the sun, even the glory of God, the highest of all, whose glory the sun of the firmament is written of as being typical" (D&C 76:62–68, 70).

Along with the Celestial Kingdom, the Doctrine and Covenants also describes the kingdoms known as Terrestrial and Telestial, represented respectively by the moon and the stars. And although all three of these areas together are what generally might be called heaven, the last two are not the places where God dwells.

Only in the Celestial Kingdom, according to the revelations, can people attain to the highest quality of life in the hereafter. In this kingdom only is there a level of spirituality which permits an association in the presence of God.

This latter environment is much like that of the Garden of Eden and the city of Enoch, or that in the premortal life. It is characterized by the type of lifestyle that might well be regarded as paradisiacal or utopian, a condition which consequently makes the cost or requirement of entry necessarily high. And yet what it amounts to is nothing more than being qualified for membership in the House of Israel, the gathering to which was a paramount belief and article of faith of the latter-day church that Joseph Smith helped to restore.

It is the requirement that a person live a good life, one that is celestial in nature, and then further qualifying by believing in Jesus Christ and obeying the principles and ordinances of the gospel. Essentially it means that he or she must develop a certain type of body or personality, one which is celestial that will be compatible with the kingdom and glory of God. "For he who is not able to abide the law of a celestial kingdom," the scripture says, "cannot abide a celestial glory" (D&C 88:22).

It is also the concept and idea that only those people who have suitably prepared themselves for the highest kingdom will feel comfortable when they get there. For them it will be a natural setting and environment in which to continue an eternal progression.

The other two kingdoms, the Terrestrial and Telestial, are also places of glory, but less important in terms of lifestyle and spiritual accomplishment. As described in the Doctrine and Covenants, these are areas that will be inhabited by people who were not as faithful in carrying out the plan of heaven and as a result will inherit a lesser award, although in regard to the glory involved, including living conditions and sociality, the record states that both will be of such a nature that surpasses all human understanding" (D&C 76:89).

At the same time, there is no question but what the Celestial Kingdom is what mankind idealistically should aspire to and anticipate, a type of glory compared to that of the sun as described in the Bible, and one also which is mentioned briefly by the Apostle Paul as a third heaven (2 Corinthians 12:2). This is the glory that prophets throughout history have referred to as a place of paradise and the kingdom of God.

It is also the supreme ideal established in the beginning before the foundation of the world and represents the highest level of achievement during premortal and earth life, everything pointing toward the Celestial Kingdom. It is the final goal and destination of all who are faithful and who aspire to membership in the House of Israel. Yet again there is always a cost involved, something everyone must do in order finally to gain entrance into the kingdom.

This is obtained generally by way of three basic steps: (1) leading a good life and developing a celestial body and personality,

(2) obeying certain rules and commandments, including baptism and a willingness to be gathered into the House of Israel, and (3) obtaining a celestialized resurrected body. The second step includes going to a temple and receiving instruction, including the reception of the highest religious ordinances.

All of these are extremely important, and yet the most vital step of all is undoubtedly the one that pertains to a good life and a celestial body. Regardless of a person's background and lineage, and whether or not he or she knows about the plan of salvation, none of these things will be of any value in a celestial sense if unaccompanied by righteous living.

Aside from any church membership, or other kinds of religious affiliation, it is a celestial type of being or personality that must be developed in order to qualify for candidacy in the highest kingdom. After that is accomplished, other requirements can be taken care of, either while a person is alive or following death and entrance into the Spirit World. The emphasis is always on good works and righteousness, along with a natural tendency to live as God lives and to strive for human kindness and perfection. All of this is the epitome of the Celestial Kingdom and a standard and ensign for all people to follow!

17

THE PLACE WHERE GOD RESIDES

Somewhere in the universe or galaxy, or whatever the right term might be, God has his residence. To many this will sound too conventional and commonplace, but it is true, or at least according to the doctrine and philosophy of the latter-day church founded upon modern revelation and the ministering of angels, which from the beginning taught that he to whom people pray is a personal God after whose image mankind was created. The church also believed that he has a resurrected body of flesh and bones and as such can physically be in only one place at a time. Again people might view these statements as inappropriately stated, regarding them to be at a level of divinity to which they are unaccustomed.

Naturally it is difficult to visualize such things as where God lives, and what he might be doing, since so very little is known about him. Also only a small amount of scripture exists that refers to this kind of subject. Yet there are certain sources of knowledge and information available, and from them a fair picture can be obtained.

First of all, there are the places in the New Testament where Jesus speaks directly to his Father, suggesting clearly that someone is in a distant place listening. Also in talking to Philip one day, it was clearly stated that anyone who had seen Jesus himself had also seen the Father, in regard to manner and appearance. Moreover, there are certain comments made by Joseph Smith at one time which provide more specific information.

"If the veil were rent today," he said, referring to the veil or curtain separating earth from heaven, "and the great God who holds this world in its orbit, and who upholds all worlds and all things by his power, was to make himself visible, I say if you were to see him today, you would see him like a man in form, like yourselves in all the person, image and very form as a man; for Adam was created in the very fashion, image, and likeness of God and received instructions from him, and walked, talked, and conversed with him, as one man talks and communes with another"[1]

These few comments, coming from a man who at the age of fourteen allegedly saw God in a grove of trees near his home is significant and noteworthy. As with prophets of old, some of whom were very young at the time, the boy experienced a heavenly vision on that occasion and learned for himself who the God of heaven is and what he looks like. In talking with Jehovah, who stood nearby, he could also tell for certain that the Father and the Son were two separate personages and had bodies much like his own, thus confirming God's statement in the Bible when he said, "Let us make man in our image, after our likeness." "So God created man in his own image," the record says, "in the image of God created he him; male and female created he them" (Genesis 1:26, 27).

For many years following the remarkable vision in the grove, Joseph Smith spoke with thousands of people, telling them what he had seen. On occasion he also mentioned the place where God resides, saying it was on a planet far removed in the universe. It has a different reckoning concerning time, he said, as does the one pertaining to angels, and is a giant orb or sphere unlike anything else in the heavens.

"The angels do not reside on a planet like this earth," he remarked, referring to the place where people live, "but they reside in the presence of God, on a globe like a sea of glass and fire, where all things for their glory are manifest, past, present, and future, and are continually before the Lord.

"The place where God resides is a great Urim and Thummim," he continued. " This earth, in its sanctified and immortal state, will be made like unto crystal and will be a Urim and Thummim to the inhabitants who dwell thereon, whereby all things pertaining to an inferior kingdom, or all kingdoms of a lower order will be manifest to those who dwell on it; and this earth will be Christ's" (D&C 130:6–9).

In regard to statements such as these, Joseph Smith was responsible for bringing a huge amount of modern scripture into existence, among which was an account pertaining to the prophet Abraham. The account is particularly interesting since it tells of a heavenly vision the ancient prophet had at one time and refers specifically to the residence and neighborhood of God.

"And I saw the stars," said Abraham, "that they were very great, and that one of them was nearest unto the throne of God; and there were many great ones which were near unto it. And the Lord said unto me: These are the governing ones; and the name of the great one is Kolob, because it is near unto me, for I am the Lord thy God: I have set this one to govern all those which belong to the same order as that upon which thou standest."

"And the Lord said unto me, by the Urim and Thummim," he said, "that Kolob was after the manner of the Lord, according to its times and seasons in the revolutions thereof; that one revolution was a day unto the Lord, after his manner of reckoning, it being one thousand years according to the time appointed unto that wheron thou standest. This is the reckoning of the Lord's time, according to the reckoning of Kolob" (Abraham 3"2–4).

In no other scripture, either ancient or modern, is there an account more remarkable and informative as this one. To

113

designate the location where God lives, as if by a system of zones and coordinates, and to identify neighboring planets, is something uncharacteristic of any other scripture. Certainly it bespeaks the knowledge and background of the man who, once again, was instrumental in bringing it into existence.

There is a multitude of modern revelation and scripture associated with Joseph Smith, including the Doctrine and Covenants and Book of Mormon, but none is more unique and outstanding than that which is associated with the prophet Abraham, recorded in a book called the Pearl of Great Price. The brief references which he makes regarding the actual planet where God resides, as well as surrounding planets, constitute a miraculous account in scripture and create a visual image that has seldom, if ever, been established. It is true that scientists can determine many of the conditions that exist in space, and what the different circumstances might be, but nothing comparable to what is attributed to Abraham occurs elsewhere in scripture. And yet it is something that might well be expressed in poetry.

Night Dream

In a dream I saw the planets and stars,
First Venus and Mercury, Jupiter and Mars,

Then millions of others arranged like jewels
Of reflected light in darkened pools.

The scene was not the common sight
That one might see on a starry night,

But a world of blue and black and gray
And moving spheres in vast array,

A world which one might only see
If once the spirit wandered free.

In rapid flight through time and space
And peopled worlds of varied race,

I moved to heavens's distant star
And viewed creation from afar.

I saw the wheel of the Milky Way,
Its hub engulfed in cosmic spray.

I saw the miracle which God has wrought
And learned the secret all men have sought.

God does not live in a distant maze
Or somewhere in a fiery blaze

But deep in the center of a group of stars,
A billion light years from Earth and Mars.[1]

Again it is noteworthy, aside from anything in prose or poetry, or in the scientific or literary world, that there is an instance in scripture which refers to the place where God lives, deep in the center of a group of stars, as it were, and an untold number of light years away. It is significant also that in the account relating to Abraham, there is a time reckoning involved, one equivalent with a statement in the Bible equating one day of God's time with one thousand years on earth (2 Peter 3:8; Psalms 90:4). Indeed, the introduction of this particular scripture during the latter days, one describing the place where God resides, constitutes a remarkable event and circumstance and is just one of many others preceding the advent and second coming of Jesus Christ!

18

THE AFTERNOON OF THE FIRST RESURRECTION

It is difficult to describe what actually might take place when Jesus returns in the clouds of heaven, clothed with power and glory. So many things will undoubtedly occur simultaneously that any chronological description is impossible. The phenomenon of millions of people on earth being caught up at the same time and billions of those who are dead coming forth from their graves is incredible and supernatural. Again it is impossible to give an adequate description of what will happen, either as to the chronology of events or otherwise.

Yet certain things stand out as evident and significant, one of them being the sudden appearance of so many children, resurrected as individuals ranging from infancy to eight years of age. An untold number will be in this immense congregation, and all of them, according to modern revelation, will be heirs to the Celestial Kingdom. There is only one specific scripture stating that children in this age group, who died early during their lifetime, will automatically return to God's presence. It is part of a revelation given to Joseph Smith and is recorded in the 137th Section of the Doctrine and Covenants.

"And I also beheld that all children who die before they arrive at the years of accountability," he said, "are saved in the Celestial Kingdom of heaven" (D&C 137:10).

This particular scripture alone will potentially have a tremendous impact on millions of people in the world today, people who heretofore have been told that unless young children are baptized, their future entrance into heaven is jeopardized. It is also a scripture, once again, that pertains meaningfully to the Second Coming. At the time that people are quickened and caught up, both the living and the dead who are righteous, their worthy children will be with them, including those who died before the age of accountability, and they will meet the Lord together as families.

The latter-day church restored by way of Joseph Smith ostensibly promoted the idea that the family was of paramount importance. Consequently, it is the one element that meaningfully binds human relationships together. And when the Lord returns in the future, it will ideally be as families that people will be there to meet him.

Only those qualifying for entrance into the celestial Kingdom of Heaven, however, will be in this group, people coming from the "four corners of the earth," the "first fruits" of the resurrection. It is only after they have made their appearance and are acknowledged by Jesus, or Jehovah, that another wave of people will then appear at an undetermined time, those mentioned in scripture as belonging to the afternoon of the first resurrection. These will be people who led good lives on earth but qualified for a kingdom of glory that was terrestrial rather than celestial.

At an unspecified time, therefore, but definitely before the predicted burning of the earth, another sound of a trumpet will be heard, much like one that occurred earlier. This will be the signal for a second phase of the resurrection to take place, now referred to as taking place in the afternoon. At this point, the righteous people who merit an inheritance in heaven that is terrestrial will come forth from their graves and resume the process of living upon the earth. And although little is known concerning this event, it will undoubtedly be an occasion of resplendency and great importance and will honor those who lived honorably and respectably during their lifetime.

A brief scripture referring to these people is recorded in the Doctrine and Covenants. "And after this," meaning the morning of the first resurrection," another angel shall sound, which is the second trump; and then cometh the redemption of those who are Christ's at his coming; who have received their part in that prison which is prepared for them, that they might receive the gospel, and be judged according to men in the flesh" (D&C 88:99).

When people die, they temporarily enter the Spirit World, and the ones who have led righteous lives go a place known as paradise, regarded also as a prison or imprisonment because for a time they are without physical bodies. During the time of the Second Coming, those who are heirs to the Celestial Kingdom will come forth during the morning of the first resurrection and be crowned with glory along with Jehovah. The people who are heirs to the Terrestrial Kingdom will come forth at a later time during the afternoon of the same resurrection. They have received their part in the prison prepared for them, referring to the time they were deprived of their bodies, and can now also be resurrected.

Concerning their circumstances in the hereafter, the Doctrine and Covenants gives the following information. "And again, we saw the terrestrial world, and behold and lo, these are they who are of the terrestrial, whose glory differs from that of the church of the Firstborn who have received the fulness of the Father, even as that of the moon differs from the sun in the firmament. Behold, these are they who died without law; and also they who are the spirits of men kept in prison, whom the Son visited, and preached the gospel unto them, that they might be judged according to men in the flesh; who received not the testimony of Jesus in the flesh, but afterwards received it.

"These are they who are honorable men of the earth, who were blinded by the craftiness of men. These are they who receive of his glory, but not of his fulness. These are they who receive of the presence of the Son, but not of the fulness of the Father. Wherefore, they are bodies terrestrial, and not bodies celestial, and differ in glory as the moon differs from the sun. These are they who are not valiant in the testimony of Jesus; wherefore, they obtain not the crown over the kingdom of our God" (D&C 76:71–79).

Regarding this information, however, specifically that which pertains to people who died without law, or a knowledge of the gospel, it is informative to remember something else in modern scripture which says that those in this particular group "who would have received it with all their hearts," had it been presented to them, would be heirs to the Celestial Kingdom rather than the Terrestrial (D&C 137:8).

Certainly these are remarkable statements and are again attributed to revelations received by Joseph Smith during his brief lifetime. They represent an extremely important time period during the morning of the first resurrection and refer to people who are now prepared to live in the Millennium. Along with those entering the Celestial Kingdom, they will enter a kingdom of their own, one relating to a life that is forever and one that is Terrestrial. Indeed, the days ahead will be a memorable time for them, and for the first time, through the power of the redemption and resurrection, they begin an entirely new kind of life, one that is Millennial and free from any misery or death, an existence with which for so long they have been associated!

19

A TIME OF JUDGMENT

Sometime following the Second Coming, an important judgment will take place, an event implied or predicted by prophets down through the centuries. In a judicial process that is again uncertain as to its chronology in time, the Lord will divide all nations, separating those who have led good lives from those who have not. In a process much like the resurrection itself, he will cause a critical division to occur which will affect all mankind.

Talking with his disciples on the Mount of Olives, Jesus referred to this event, using sheep and goats as a way of explanation and instruction. "When the Son of Man shall come in his glory," he said, "and all the holy angels with him, then shall he sit upon the throne of his glory: and before him shall be gathered all nations: and he shall separate them one from another, as a shepherd divideth his sheep from the goats: and he shall set the sheep on his right hand, but the goats on the left" (Matthew 25:31–33).

In a massive judgment comprising all nations and a countless number people, Jehovah will conduct and transact a solemn ceremony, one which will be a day of vengeance for many people because of wrongdoing, and yet otherwise for those who have led righteous lives. This will be an occasion, according to modern

121

scripture, where the Lord will appear as though clothed in dyed garments. "And it shall be said:" the record says, "Who is this that cometh down from God in heaven with dyed garments; yea, from the regions which are not known, clothed in his glorious apparel, traveling in the greatness of his strength? And he shall say: I am he who spake in righteousness, mighty to save.

And the Lord shall be red in his apparel, and his garments like him that treadeth in the wine-vat. And so great shall be the glory of his presence that the sun shall hide his face in shame, and the moon shall withhold its light, and the stars shall be hurled from their places. And his voice shall be heard: I have trodden the winepress alone, and have brought judgment upon all people; and none were with me; and I have trampled them in my fury, and I did tread upon them in mine anger, and their blood have I sprinkled upon my garments, and stained all my raiment; for this was the day of vengeance which was in my heart" (Revelation 20:12–14).

In regard to the Second Coming, the Apostle Paul also referred to a time of judgment. "For we must all appear before the judgment seat of Christ," he said, "that every one may receive the things done in his body, according to that he hath done, whether it be good or bad" (2 Corinthians 5:10).

Ironically, the Doctrine and Covenants says very little concerning the day of judgment, except to warn that it is imminent and about to take place. It does refer, however, to something significantly related, namely the secret acts of men and the thoughts and intents of their hearts, as well as the mighty works of God, all of which are outlined according to the seven dispensations of time that are so prominent in the annals of scripture.

"And again, another angel shall sound his trump," the scripture says, "which is the seventh angel, saying: It is finished; it is finished! The Lamb of God hath overcome and trodden the wine-press alone, even the wine-press of the wrath of Almighty God. And then shall the angels be crowned with the glory of his might, and the saints shall be filled with his glory, and receive their inheritance and be made equal with him.

"And then shall the first angel again sound his trump in the ears of all living, and reveal the secret acts of men, and the mighty works of God in the first thousand years. And then shall the second angel sound his trump, and reveal the secret acts of men, and the thoughts and intents of their hearts, and the mighty works of God in the second thousand years—and so on, until the seventh angel shall sound his trump; and he shall stand forth upon the land and upon the sea, and swear in the name of him who sitteth upon the throne, that there shall be time no longer; and Satan shall be bound, that old serpent, who is called the devil, and shall not be loosed for the space of a thousand years" (D&C 88:106–110).

The thousand years, of course, refers to the time of the Millennium, at the end of which will be the final battle between Michael the archangel and Lucifer, also known as the devil, as well as the completion of seven thousand years of the earth's continuance, or its temporal existence. But the significant thing in this particular scripture is a reference to the thoughts and intents of the hearts of men, which in turn is reminiscent of another scripture related to the day of judgment. The latter was recorded by Joseph Smith in relation to a vision he received soon after the restoration of the latter-day church, which was eventually to be called the Church of Jesus Christ of Latter-day Saints.

"Thus came the voice of the Lord unto me," he said, "saying all who would have died without a knowledge of this gospel, who would have received it if they had been permitted to tarry, shall be heirs to the Celestial Kingdom of God; and all that shall die henceforth without a knowledge of it, who would have received it with all their hearts, shall be heirs of that kingdom; for I, the Lord, will judge all men according to their works, according to the desires of their hearts" (D&C 137:7).

This last statement appears to be saying in essence that mankind, in the process of living, is judging itself by the way they live. According to their works and according to the desires of their hearts, they make it unnecessary in a meaningful way for the Lord to make any kind of final judgment. It is the idea again that a person needs to lead a good life, one where he or she is righteous and worthy and can qualify for entrance into the Celestial Kingdom. It is also the concept that only those who have suitably prepared themselves for the highest kingdom will feel comfortable when they get there.

Certainly the Judgment coming in the future for all men and women is much like the Second Coming itself. For those who anticipate it and look forward to it, and have prepared themselves, it will be a time of gladness and rejoicing. For those who have done otherwise, it will undoubtedly be a much different time. Yet it is something that has been predicted and prophesied down through the ages by inspired prophets of God and in its own due time will eventually happen!

20

Holocaust and Burning

A strategic revelation in the Doctrine and Covenants states that "in the beginning of the seventh thousand years will the Lord God sanctify the earth, and complete the salvation of man, and judge all things, and shall redeem all things, except that which he hath not put into his power, when he shall have sealed all things, unto the end of all things" (D&C 77:12). Surely there are few scriptures that can equal the significance of this one. In only a few steps, it lists the main events that will take place at the time of the Second Coming.

These include (1) a final judgment, (2) the redemption of all things, (3) completion of the salvation of man, (4) a sealing of all things, whatever they happen to be, and (5) the sanctification of the earth. The last step will be the burning and cleansing, preparatory to the earth receiving its paradisiacal glory and eventually death and resurrection, following which it will become the abode of those inheriting the Celestial Kingdom.

But first the earth must be burned. Every corruptible thing must be incinerated and destroyed. As in the days of Noah when all living things perished except those that were in the ark, so it will be that at the end of the world, all corruptible things on the face of the earth being burned with fire. A massive cleansing will occur at that time, and the earth's surface will be sterilized and purified.

Then will the prayer of a personified earth, as recorded in modern scripture, be fulfilled, a prayer saying, "Wo, wo is me, the mother of men; I am pained, I am weary, because of the wickedness of my children. When shall I rest, and be cleansed from the filthiness which is gone forth out of me? When will my Creator sanctify me, that I may rest, and righteousness for a season abide upon my face?" (Moses 7:48).

Certainly a tremendous event will take place on the occasion of the earth's burning. It will be a time that not only fulfills religious prophecy but also performs a sacred ordinance. Again it will be as in the days of Noah when the earth was baptized in water by immersion. Now in the latter days, in the Saturday evening of time, it will be baptized again, by fire and the Holy Ghost; born again, as it were, "of water and of the Spirit" (John 3:5).

It is difficult to visualize what will happen when much of the earth's surface is burned with fire. An account of a mass burning or holocaust might be understandable, yet it is difficult to comprehend. "For, behold, the day cometh," the Bible says, quoting the prophet Malachi, "that shall burn as an oven; and all the proud, yea, and all that do wickedly shall be stubble: and the day that cometh shall burn them up, saith the Lord of hosts, that it shall leave them neither root nor branch" (Malachi 4:1).

Referring to unrighteous people, Isaiah records that "they shall be as stubble; the fire shall burn them; they shall not deliver themselves from the power of the flame: there shall not be a coal to warm at, nor fire to sit before it" (Isaiah 47:14).

In a further scripture from the Bible, a letter written by Paul to the Thessalonians, the apostle states, "And to you who are troubled rest with us, when the Lord Jesus shall be revealed from heaven with his mighty angels, in flaming fire taking vengeance on them that know not God, and obey not the gospel of our Lord

Jesus Christ: who shall be punished with everlasting destruction from the presence of the Lord, and from the glory of his power" (2 Thessalonians 1:7–9).

At the precise time of the Second Coming, however, the morning of the First Resurrection will take place prior to any devastation or burning. This is the time when people living on earth and people in their graves will be caught up in order to meet the Lord and descend with him, people coming forth "from the four quarters of the earth." Then will come the afternoon of the First Resurrection, as well as the completion of the salvation of man, referring to the periods of judgment, redemption, and sealing. According to modern revelation, it is only at this time that the worldwide burning across the earth will occur. "Then shall the arm of the Lord fall upon the nations," the scripture says (D&C 45:47).

Again the chronology of events is not always clear, but the occurrences involved during this time seem generally to be in place. The time of burning and the consequent sanctification of the earth appear to be the concluding events, those prior to what might be called the beginning of the Millennium. And yet the magnitude of what will happen is still something beyond comprehension, as well as a cause of apprehension for many people.

It is interesting to note in the Doctrine and Covenants what the Lord says people ought to be doing in regard to his Second Coming and the catastrophic burning which lies ahead. "Behold, it is my will," he says, "that all they who call upon my name, and worship me according to mine everlasting gospel, should gather together, and stand in holy places; and prepare for the revelation which is to come, when the veil of the covering of my temple, in my tabernacle, which hideth the earth, shall be taken off, and all flesh shall see me together.

"And every corruptible thing, both of man, or of the beasts of the field, or of the fowls of the heavens, or of the fish of the sea, that dwells upon all the face of the earth, shall be consumed; and

127

also that of element shall melt with fervent heat; and all things shall become new, that my knowledge and glory may dwell upon all the earth" (D&C 101:22–25).

"Behold, now it is called today until the coming of the son of Man," the scriptures say, "and verily it is a day of sacrifice, and a day for the tithing of my people; for he that is tithed shall not be burned at his coming. For after today cometh the burning—this is speaking after the manner of the Lord—for verily I say, tomorrow all the proud and they that do wickedly shall be as stubble; and I will burn them up, for I am the Lord of hosts; and I will not spare any that remain in Babylon. Wherefore, if ye believe me, ye will labor while it is called today" (D&C 64:23–25).

Surely it is today that people need to be concerned with as far as a future burning is concerned. Today is the time to prepare and be ready. Angels above are no longer just waiting but have allegedly left the portals of heaven and are now pouring out judgments upon the earth.[1] The time is definitely drawing closer for the biblical parable pertaining to the wheat and the tares to be fulfilled, and what is happening in the world today is an obvious sign of the times.

There is only one place in the Bible that tells about the wheat and the tares, that which is recorded in the gospel of Matthew. When tares began growing in a wheat field, for example, the servants asked the householder if they should remove them, but he told them to wait, saying otherwise they would root up some of the wheat with them. "Let both grow together until the harvest," he said, "and in the time of harvest I will say to the reapers, Gather ye together first the tares, and bind them in bundles to burn them: but gather the wheat into my barn" (Matthew 13:30).

The tares in the future, of course, are the wayward people of the world that will perish in the fiery holocaust. But modern scripture, in interpreting and rephrasing this account, states that the wheat will first be gathered into the barn, after which the tares will then be gathered and bound in bundles to be burned.

"Behold, verily I say unto you," the record says, "the angels are crying unto the Lord day and night, who are ready and waiting to be sent forth to reap down the fields." "Therefore, let the wheat and the tares grow together until the harvest is fully ripe; then ye shall first gather out the wheat from among the tares, and after the gathering of the wheat, behold and lo, the tares are bound in bundles, and the field remaineth to be burned." (D&C 86:5, 7). The idea is that before angels commence the fiery blaze, the righteous will be separated from those who are unworthy, while missionaries go among the people trying to save all who are willing to listen.

It is interesting to learn about the angels involved, which some might consider to be figurative or symbolic, whereas in reality they are more likely actual individuals in charge of future operations originating in heaven, mentioned not only in the book of Revelation in the Bible but also in modern revelation.

The biblical record refers to four angels standing on the four corners of the earth, holding the four winds of the earth and controlling whether or not they will be harmful or destructive. Another angel then appears, ascending from the east, crying "with a loud voice to the four angels, to whom it was given to hurt the earth and the sea, saying, Hurt not the earth, neither the sea, nor the trees, till we have sealed the servants of our God in their foreheads. And I heard the number of them which were sealed: and there were sealed an hundred and forty four thousand of all the tribes of the children of Israel" (Revelation 7:1–4).

In regard to the four angels, modern revelation gives the following information: "We are to understand that they are four angels sent forth from God, to whom is given power over the four parts of the earth, to save life or to destroy; these are they who have the everlasting gospel to commit to every nation, kindred, tongue and people; having power to shut up the heavens, to seal up unto life, or to cast down to the regions of darkness."

Next an explanation is given as to the identity of the angel coming from the east. "We are to understand," the scripture says," that the angel ascending from the east is he to whom is given the seal of the living God over the twelve tribes of Israel; wherefore, he crieth unto the four angels having the everlasting gospel, saying: Hurt not the earth, neither the sea, nor the trees, till we have sealed the servants of our God in their foreheads."

And finally there is the revelation identifying the 144,000 people who have a seal placed in the foreheads. "We are to understand that those who are sealed are high priests, ordained unto the holy order of God, to administer the everlasting gospel; for they are they who are ordained out of every nation, kindred, tongue, and people, by the angels to whom is given power over the nations of the earth, to bring as many as will come to the church of the Firstborn" (D&C 77:8–9, 11).

Information in the Bible, therefore, is again clarified by modern scripture, telling how in the future a huge band of missionaries, no less than an army of high priests, will go among the people of the earth, gathering out the wheat, as it were, before the four angels in charge give the signal to start burning the tares. Ordained ministers of the gospel, possessing an Israelite connection and representing the tribes of Israel, will travel throughout the world in the most extensive proselyting program that has ever been conducted. Each will be endowed with a divine commission and priesthood authority and will personally represent the Lord Jesus Christ!

"Therefore, I must gather together my people," the Lord says, "according to the parable of the wheat and the tares, that the wheat may be secured in the garners to possess eternal life, and be crowned with celestial glory, when I shall come in the kingdom of my Father to reward every man according as his work shall be; while the tares shall be bound in bundles, and their bands made strong, that they may be burned with unquenchable fire" (D&C 101:65–66).

Certainly the burning of the earth at this time will be an inherent part of the ultimate climax at the end of the world, not occurring simultaneously with the Second Coming and the First Resurrection but apparently a short time after. It will necessarily be a time of sadness and remorse for billions of people, those whose resurrection will be delayed for a thousand years and who are heirs to a Telestial Kingdom of glory. But at the same time it will be a time of gladness and happiness for the ones who inherit the higher kingdoms and enjoy the benefits of a new kind of earth, one that is sanctified and renewed with a paradisiacal glory. Indeed it will be a bright new world for all who have led good lives and carried out the plan that was designed in heaven. It will be a reward for a job well done as righteous people now look forward to the Millennium!

Notes

1. Bruce R. McConkie, *Mormon Doctrine* (Salt Lake City: Bookcraft) 178.

21

In the Millennium

Several events in scripture have been referred to as the beginning of the Second Coming, including the Savior's visit to Adam-ondi-Ahman, his appearance on the Mount of Olives during the Battle of Armageddon, and when he stands upon Mount Zion with 144,000 missionaries. The more traditional reference to this remarkable occurence, however, is the exact point in time when the curtain of heaven is opened and the face of the Lord is revealed, the moment when he descends in clouds of glory bringing a host of angels with him. It is also at this time that righteous people living on earth who are heirs to the Celestial Kingdom, as well as all of the righteous dead, will be caught up to meet him.

This last event has also been designated as the beginning of the Millennium. The first public appearance of Jehovah, aside from earlier ones that have been more private, is the traditional date for the commencement of one thousand years of world peace. It does not refer to the beginning of the seventh millennium, but rather to the era known as the Millennium, spelled with a capital letter, a period of time occurring at a subsequent date

As to the actual commencement of this time period, however, which traditionally is one with no death or sorrow, it will logically not take place until after the predicted fire and burning. The incomparable entrance of Jehovah and the company of angels will be a resplendent time of joy and gladness, but in the background will be a worldwide scene of mortality, unrighteous people living on earth and destined to inherit the Telestial Kingdom. This implies that the actual Millennium will follow the time of holocaust and burning, at a time subsequent to when the earth is cleansed and restored to a paradisiacal state which existed anciently in the Garden of Eden.

Certainly this will be period of time in history that righteous people in all eras and ages have anticipated and looked forward to. To good people everywhere, whose morality and way of living have been in accordance with heaven's plan, it is a natural goal and destiny. The pathway to the kingdom of heaven that Jesus talked about is sometimes long and tedious, but for those whose natural inclination is to do good and avoid wrong doing, the goal ahead, including the Millennium, is a natural one and a manner of life to which they will be well suited and accustomed.

The Millennium itself will be characterized by many things that are different from mortality, possibly the most evident being the absence of death and sorrow. These will no longer be a factor in daily living, and people will have an entirely new perspective and viewpoint, particularly a more vivid concept concerning the future. No longer is there to be hesitancy or doubt regarding the hereafter, and the goal ahead will be finding happiness in whatever kingdom and glory has been prepared.

The fact that death as formerly experienced on earth is forever in the past will especially be comforting and significant. People will still continue to be born into mortality and live upon the earth as mortal human beings, yet when they reach a certain age and it is time for them to make a change, they will die and be changed to immortality in the twinkling of an eye, gaining entrance into whatever kingdom has been prepared for them.

"In that day an infant shall not die until he is old; and his life shall be as the age of a tree; and when he dies he shall not sleep, that is to say in the earth, but shall be changed in the twinkling of an eye, and shall be caught up, and his rest shall be glorious" (D&C 101:30–31).

The same will be true at the time of the Second Coming. "And he that liveth when the Lord shall come, and hath kept the faith, blessed is he; nevertheless, it is appointed to him to die at the age of man. Wherefore, children shall grow up until they become old; old men shall die; but they shall not sleep in the dust, but they shall be changed in the twinkling of an eye" (D&C 63:50–51).

A promise also will be realized at this time which says that righteous parents will have the opportunity of raising children during the Millennium who died prematurely. The resurrected offspring will then grow to the full stature of their spirits and prime of life, whatever that age might be. Then at the appropriate time, they will instantly be changed from mortality to immortality and, like their parents, be caught up to enter into their respective kingdoms. All of this will take place according to the mercy and justice of a heavenly Father.

Indeed, the Millennium will be an extraordinary and miraculous period of time, a utopia which has been advertised and predicted to one degree or another for six millennia. It will be a time of literal peace on earth when the enmity of all flesh comes to an end, including that which exists in the animal kingdom where even the most ferocious beasts will dwell together in harmony. A utopian reality will finally be realized as the lion and the lamb lie down together without any ire. Certainly this latter scene is a traditional symbol of the Millennium itself.

It will be characteristic of the Millennium for people now to be living separate and apart from any who are of a telestial nature. For the first time since Adam and Eve left the garden of Eden, people of either a celestial or terrestrial disposition will be living together in harmony. Everyone will not as yet be accepting Jehovah as the Son of God, as people continue in their individual beliefs and philosophies, but sometime during the thousand years to follow, all will eventually come to a knowledge of the truth and confess that Jesus is the Christ.

In the meantime, people will continue to be born as they did earlier. Millions of persons who had formerly been spirit children of God living in his presence will come to earth to gain experience and work out their salvation. It is almost beyond comprehension to visualize what will occur during the coming centuries as a countless number of people transfer to earth, pass through a mortal probation, and then in a twinkling of an eye be resurrected and enter a respective kingdom, whether it be celestial or terrestrial. Those in the Celestial Kingdom will go to a select place on or near the planet where God resides, and those in the Terrestrial apparently to some other planet in the universe.

At the same time, the population of the House of Israel will continue to expand. The institution that became well known during the time of Abraham, Isaac, and Jacob and became a great nation in the Middle East during the time of Saul, David, and Solomon will now be an important factor in the time of the hereafter. An Israelite presence will continue to exist as people qualify and enter the Celestial Kingdom, perpetuating what has been called the Gathering of Israel. In no place in the annals of scripture, whether it be ancient or modern, is there a concept more basic and representative than this one, signifying the progression of righteous people throughout the ages of time, from premortality in the distant past to mortality on a telestial earth, and then into the time of the Millennium and hereafter!

22

THE HOUSE OF ISRAEL

One way of viewing the House of Israel is to visualize three houses instead of just one. In the lifetime prior to the creation of the earth, for example, one which might be termed premortality, the spirit children of God progressed in many different ways. By way of agency and aptitude, they developed in a wide spectrum of accomplishment in a wide variety of fields, not only in areas such as art, literature, and science, but also those pertaining to religion and moral behavior. In the development of a well-rounded personality or character, many traits were important, but the most important as far as the Lord was concerned was undoubtedly religion. Consequently, obedience to a plan organized in heaven by Deity was of paramount importance, and those who subscribed to it constituted the first House of Israel, or an institution comparable to it.

When the time came for them to transfer to earth and receive physical bodies, they were positioned or located according to a specific plan, the more preferable areas generally being given to those who had been obedient in heaven, the people who were members of the House of Israel. It was the idea that in this kind of situation, they would have a better opportunity of succeeding on earth and carrying out heaven's plan. A scriptural basis for this idea is found in two places in the Bible, the first of which is in the book of Deuteronomy.

"Remember the days of old," the scripture says, "consider the years of many generations: ask thy father, and he will shew thee; thy elders, and they will tell thee. When the most High divided to the nations their inheritance, when he separated the sons of Adam, he set the bounds of the people according to the number of the children of Israel. For the Lord's portion is his people; Jacob is the lot of his inheritance" (Deuteronomy 32:7–9).

A paraphrase of this might also be stared as follows: When the most High divided to the nations their inheritance, when he separated the sons of Adam, he established the lineages and set the bounds of the people according to whether or not they were members of the House of Israel.

A similar scripture is found in the book of Acts in the New Testament where the Apostle Paul in speaking to the Athenians states that God "giveth to all life, and breath, and all things; and hath made of one blood all nations of men for to dwell on all the face of the earth, and hath determined the times before appointed and the bounds of their habitation" (Acts 17:25–26).

Reference to the location and bounds of people being transferred to earth, therefore, as well as their time of transfer, is specifically outlined in scripture. An index or basic formula was established relating to the children of Israel, one associated with their premortal life, the long era of time before the earth was created. This means that people who lived righteously from the time of Adam to the time of Jacob, the grandson of Abraham, were theoretically part of the "children of Israel" referred to in scripture. During the time of mortality, after Jacob's name was changed to Israel, his progeny specifically was called by that name, all righteous people together belonging to the second House of Israel.

In the late 10th Century B.C., the House of Israel, consisting of the tribes of Jacob and their descendants, separated into two groups or kingdoms. The quarreling that occurred following the death of Solomon finally took its toll, and the house remained permanently divided. During subsequent centuries, both kingdoms were conquered by invading armies, however, and the people were scattered in many directions, a dispersion that was not only geographic but one also that was spiritual, as people departed from the teachings of Jehovah. Thus occurred what has been called the Scattering of Israel, a phenomenon referred to in both ancient and modern scripture and one which continued for hundreds of years until the concept of Israel relatively became nonexistent.

Then came the time of restoration in the latter days when the man known as Joseph Smith made his appearance. As a boy he received the remarkable vision in a grove near his home, and thereafter the era of ministering of angels was instituted. One angel after another appeared in succession, each conferring authority and ordinances pertaining to the gospel, one of which pertained to the restoration of a church that had existed anciently during the time of Christ and another to the ten tribes and the gathering of Israel.

In the new church of the latter days, incoming converts were designated by divine revelation as Israelites, an action which commenced the beginning of the third House of Israel. As a consequence, the phenomenon of the Gathering of Israel again came into existence. A concept that eventually would spread throughout the world now became an important part of the gospel, and missionaries eventually became engaged in a worldwide program of proselyting.

The idea was that Israel was now being gathered again in order to provide general welfare and religious instruction for members. It was a process that would continue into the Millennium. From the very beginning, it counseled people how to live in the present as well as the future, at the same time preparing them for the second coming of Jesus Christ.

Important in all of this was the role of the latter-day Church. As in former times, it was guided and administered by apostles and prophets acting under the supervision of Christ, or Jehovah, although following the Second Coming it will be in the era of time known as Millennial. The organization of leadership will very possibly be much the same as before with the idea and concept of a triumvirate predominating.

A triumvirate, as a type of administration and leadership, is government by three persons who share authority and responsibility. It is a commission or ruling body of three made famous in history by the ancient Romans. The original prototype, however, is the Holy Trinity itself, the Godhead of the universe where God the Father and Jesus Christ and the Holy Ghost are supreme.

The revelations of Joseph Smith regarding church government in the latter-day church stated that there should be a First Presidency consisting of three individuals, assisted by a Quorum of Twelve Apostles and other designated officials. This was in accordance with one of the church's creeds which claimed a belief in the same organization that existed in the primitive church.

Consequently, the church as it was organized in the years prior to the Millennium consisted of many priesthood and auxiliary officers that were three in number, whether it was a president and two counselors or a superintendent and two assistants. The concept of a triumvirate was always noticeably present. It is interesting also that the principal officers outlined in the American Constitution, claimed by Joseph Smith to be divinely inspired, follow the same format.

The executive branch of government, for example, is comparable to the first member of the Godhead, or ruling head, with the legislative or law-making branch is associated with Jehovah, the supreme lawgiver on Mount Sinai of the Old Testament. This leaves the Holy Ghost who is likened to the judicial department for any number of reasons. It is an interesting and significant comparison.

This relates also to a situation existing in heaven where there are three separate kingdoms or glories. Moreover, it is reminiscent of what Jesus told his apostles the night before he died. "In my Father's house are many mansions:" he said, on that occasion, "if it were not so I would have told you" (John 14:2). Certainly the concept of the triumvirate itself is significant as it relates to the kingdoms of heaven which are Celestial, Terrestrial, or Telestial.

Presumably it will also be a factor with people living on earth during the Millennium. Those in mortality who abide by a celestial or terrestrial law, for example, will be living together, and their systems of organization in government and otherwise will very likely be similar to those that existed earlier. Much of what takes place at the beginning of the Millennial period, in fact, might not be too different from that with which modern society is already accustomed.

An untold number of people numbering in the millions or billions will continue to be born on earth in those days, coming from premortality and taking their own place in the stream of history. Death will no longer be a factor, but problems and challenges will still occur, all necessary in character building and human development. There will also be the countless choices people will make as to how to conduct their lives in all facets of societal living, including matters of religion. The Millennium, in fact, will be a time when people have their own church or religious affiliation and will make decisions based on personal belief and philosophy. And among these is one in particular that must be made by the Jewish people whose query since the meridian of time has been whether or not Jesus was the Son of God.

An important example of this is a singular event that most likely will occur sometime following the morning and afternoon of the First Resurrection, after the burning of the earth has taken place, as Jewish people approach Jesus on one occasion and ask him a question. "What are these wounds in thine hands?" they say in wonderment, after which his answer will be, "Those with which I was wounded in the house of my friends" (Zechariah 13:6).

The scriptural account of this event is very brief, occurring abruptly in the book of Zechariah in the Old Testament in the midst of what appears to be very irrelevant material. And although the text obviously refers to Jesus, it still leaves unanswered questions, and it remains for the Doctrine and Covenants once again to give an explanation and clarification.

"And then shall the Jews look upon me," the record says, "and say: What are these wounds in thine hands and in thy feet? Then shall they know that I am the Lord; for I will say unto them: These wounds are the wounds with which I was wounded in the house of my friends. I am he who was lifted up. I am Jesus that was crucified. I am the Son of God. And then shall they weep because of their iniquities; then shall they lament because they persecuted their king" (D&C 45:51–53).

It will be a brief interlude in time when the plight of the Jewish people is once more brought to the forefront. Again it is similar to the humorous question a person might ask upon seeing Jesus for the first time: "Sir, is this your first visit, or your second?" Yet, it is also a serious commentary, as well as censure and condemnation, concerning the many centuries the Jewish people themselves have been criticized and persecuted for one thing after another. Surely their plight is one of the most notable instances of social bias and prejudice throughout history.

In the ancient record Joseph Smith translated, resulting in the Book of Mormon, a particular scripture occurs in which a prophet named Nephi censures the Gentiles, or non-Jewish people, for their social attitude, specifically when they say they already have a Bible and have no need for another. This was with the understanding that the Bible itself originally came from the ancestors of the Jews.

"And what thank they the Jews for the Bible which they receive from them?" Nephi asks, speaking for the Lord. "Yea, what do the Gentiles mean? Do they remember the travels, and the labors, and the pains of the Jews, and their diligence unto me, in bringing forth salvation unto the Gentiles?

"O ye Gentiles, have you remembered the Jews, mine ancient covenant people? Nay; but ye have cursed them, and have hated them, and have not sought to recover them. But behold, I will return all these things upon your own heads; for I the Lord have not forgotten my people" (2 Nephi 29:4–5).

Statements such as these are a further condemnation of any who criticize or demean the Jewish people, regardless of how they feel about Jesus Christ. They are representative of another ancient prophet called Mormon who more than sixteen centuries ago spoke vehemently in behalf of the Jews. "Yea, and ye need not any longer hiss, nor spurn, nor make game of the Jews," he said, "nor any of the remnant of the house of Israel; for behold, the Lord remembereth his covenant unto them, and he will do unto them according to that which he hath sworn" (3 Nephi 29:8).

Indeed these are events and circumstances, among many others, that may well relate to a time in the future when the Lord returns in the clouds of heaven to judge all people according to their works and the attitudes they have toward one another. As in the past, these people will face the challenge, as well as the opportunity, of living in a large composite society, consisting of different races, nationalities, and backgrounds, as well as personal beliefs. And yet for the first time, it will be a very different kind of society which possesses a higher standard of morality, one that is celestial or terrestrial.

Another noticeable difference will be the presence of people in society who have been resurrected, residing for indefinite periods of time. Although these will not be permanent residents, they apparently will visit from time to time for whatever purpose. Joseph Smith alluded to this on one occasion when he spoke of the Millennium saying, "Christ and the resurrected saints will reign over the earth during the thousand years. They will not probably dwell upon the earth, but will visit it when they please, or when it is necessary to govern it."[1]

An important promise made to righteous people who are heirs to the Celestial Kingdom is that someday they can participate in the administration of affairs in the House of Israel. Not only will they be joint heirs of glory with God and Jehovah but will assist in many ways pertaining to the kingdom, helping to rule and reign, as it were. Surely it is a noble thought, and for those who prove worthy, it will be a significant aspect of immortality and eternal life.

Yet regarding what will actually happen, one thing remains clear, and that is that a millennium or one thousand years is an awfully long time, and any normal reflection on this time period might well cause a person to wonder what he or she will be doing. A normal lifetime of less that a hundred years is one thing, but what about ten times that long, as well as eternity beyond?

What lies in store for those who inherit the Celestial Kingdom as they enter the Millennium, and what might a person's contemplations be? One example expressed in poetry shows a humorous anecdote where the person involved hesitates momentarily and maybe for the first time wonders seriously about lies ahead.

The Millennium

We wait for the Millennium
And the thousand years of peace,
But when it comes,
What will we do
When the new wears off?[2]

A serious commentary on the future, however, regarding the status of people in whatever kingdom of glory they might be, is the surprising revelation in scripture concerning those who inherit the very lowest of glory, namely that which is telestial. "And thus we saw , in the heavenly vision," the scripture says, recorded by Joseph Smith and a man named Sidney Rigdon, "the glory of the telestial, which surpasses all understanding; and no man knows it except him to whom God has revealed it" (D&C 76:89–90).

Even those in the lowest kingdom will experience outstanding societal living. There need be no hesitancy, therefore, as to what lies ahead. Wherever it might be, and whatever kingdom in involved, people are destined to enjoy that part of heaven where they are placed, many of them regretting they had not done better. Again as recorded in scripture, what occurs at that time will surpass all understanding.

This essentially might be inferred from the promise given in the Bible, stated by the Apostle Paul in a letter to the Corinthians. "But as it is written," he said, "eye hath not seen, nor ear heard, neither have entered into the heart of man, the things which God hath prepared for them that love him" (1 Corinthians 2:9). The same thing had been declared by Isaiah hundreds of years earlier. "For since the beginning of the world," the prophet said, "men have not heard, nor perceived by the ear, neither hath the eye seen, O God, before thee, what he hath prepared for him that waiteth for him" (Isaiah 64:4).

Nothing could be more optimistic and reassuring, as well as just and merciful, than what is found in these particular scriptures. They describe a reward and manner of life which God will provide for all people, except a very few for whom there will be no reward or glory at all. Indeed, they are an important preface and introduction for people of the world as they contemplate and prepare for the future.

In the commencement of the Millennium, therefore, and after six millennia on earth, people finally arrive at the threshold of a new era of human history and an additional one thousand years, with many people yet to be born. At that memorable moment in time, there will be an ultimate climax in which one dispensation closes and another one begins. A tremendous stream of humanity finally reaches a point where regular human history comes to a conclusion and a very different one takes its place, the Lord Jehovah for the first time reigning personally upon the earth following his Second Coming, and a triumphant earth, after being renewed, obtaining its paradisiacal glory!

Notes

1. Joseph Fielding Smith (ed.), *Teachings of the Prophet Joseph Smith* (Salt Lake City: Deseret Book), 155, 268.

2. Clay McConkie, *Fields of Sunshine* (Springville: Bonneville Books), 42.

ABOUT THE AUTHOR

Clay McConkie is a native of Utah. He received a BA from Brigham Young University and an MA and PhD from the University of Utah. He taught in the Salt Lake City schools for thirty years. He and his wife reside in Provo, Utah, and they are the parents of four children.

Clay is also the author of *One Flesh, The Gathering of the Waters, The Ten Lost Tribes, In Ephraim's Footsteps, In His Father's Image, 600 B.C., The Final Countdown, A Man Named Peleg,* and *Fields of Sunshine.*